CHECKMATE

A Sri Lankan Story

An interwoven story of two families.
A saga of mystery, manipulation
and murder.

Nilu A

DEDICATION

Dedicated to my beloved *father*.

Mohammed Lebbe Marrikar Aboosally

Acknowledgement

To my dearest husband **Zarkir** and my beloved **children** for their continuous encouragement and support.

And to the two Grand ladies...

The late Mrs **Mildred Gunawardena** for being the initial source of inspiration.

Mrs **Padma Nanayakkara** for being my source of information on life in Sri Lanka from the 1920s to the 1950s.

Contents

Contents • 7

PART ONE – WHITE

Chapter One

The Opening Gambit

It was past the midnight hour.

It was the time the locals believed ghosts, ghouls, and spirits roamed the lonely roads. At a sharp bend in the road, the driver hit the brakes, and the car came to a sudden halt. She was a brave lady, but the unexpected stop unnerved her. She peered in the direction Sirisena had his gaze fixated upon, and through the rain-splattered window, she saw a little child seated alone by the side of the road.

Mrs Agnes Elizabeth Wijenayake was travelling back to the capital city of Colombo after visiting her estates on the southern coast of the island. This was an annual occurrence, and it was not unusual for her to commence her journey at night after an early dinner. Yet, on this night, her journey had been unexpectedly delayed. Stormy weather conditions, accompanied by strong winds, had uprooted a large tree and caused an obstruction on the coastal route she usually took to return to the capital.

Sirisena, her long-serving old driver had suggested the alternate inland route and rather than abort her journey, she had made the decision to proceed along the lonely road he had mentioned. To be fair to Sirisena, the weather was clear when they diverted to the alternate route. She was not of a nervous disposition and was used to travelling late at night, accompanied by only the old driver.

The weather had changed an hour into the journey. The storm hit. The skies opened up. Sirisena inched forward, crawling along the narrow windy road. Dark vegetation fringed the roads, transforming the alternate route into a treacherous one. There was no street lighting, not one shop or residence in slght; in fact, it had been over an hour since they had last sighted any sign of human habitation. She felt rather than heard the howling winds outside, the swaying branches of trees brushing against the closed windows. The heavy raindrops flowed in sheets down the windscreen, making visibility impossible.

Yet, she did not hesitate an instant as she bade Sirisena to stop and check on the child, but Sirisena had frozen into stone. He sat rooted in his seat, his dark complexion ashen, beads of sweat dripping down his face as he chanted prayers invoking all the gods, interspersed with the words "Holman, Holman," whispered under his breath.

The child had not moved, still seated in the same spot. She opened the door of the car and stepped out into the pouring rain. The child was real—flesh and blood, dazed, alone, soaked, and shivering in shock. She scooped the little one in her arms, climbed back into the vehicle, and commanded Sirisena to drive to the nearest hospital or police station. Her loud voice resurrected Sirisena back to life as he resumed driving without even once looking back or uttering a single word.

The little child, barely older than an infant, clung to her damp body for as much warmth or comfort as she offered but made not a whimper or sound.

Chapter Two

The Ivory Castle/"Ath Dhal Walawe"

A low wall with elaborate lotus motif mouldings ran around the property. On both ends of the wall stood two massive gate posts, each crowned with a carved elephant head. The wall itself served more as a decorative feature to mark the boundaries rather than a deterrent to keep people out. The ornamental grilled gate had been a relatively recent addition, as in the days gone by, the entrance to this residence had always been open to all.

A long sandy road led straight up and then divided into semi-circular paths to enclose the house. The road ran to the rear, where you came upon three massive barns. These barns had stored the coconuts and rice grains cultivated in the surrounding fields belonging to the owners of the residence. The barns had the capacity to ensure enough grain could be stored to feed the entire village for at least a year in times of drought. Today it served more as storerooms for discarded furniture or as garages to house the vehicles.

Low temple trees lined the sandy roads leading up to the house. In the garden at the front of the house sat a large circular man-made pond filled with lotus blooms. An occasional peacock could be seen strutting around the garden, and if one was lucky enough, one might even witness one dancing.

The original house was built in 1840 as a simple three-roomed bungalow, with additions and renovations over the many subsequent years. The house of today stands on flat ground within a coconut plantation of around fifty acres. It is a sprawling single-storey structure containing fourteen bedrooms set around two vast indoor courtyards.

An ancient carved moonstone lies beneath the four steps leading up to the house's entrance. A sturdy entrance door made out of a single plank of teak wood opens into a large reception area. Two pairs of giant elephant tusks mounted on solid ebony frames dominate both ends of this vast hall. These matching pairs of tusks are famous throughout the island for being the longest ones on record.

Open verandahs run the length of the house on either side. The edges of the tiled roof, the borders around the windows, and the panels above the doors are framed by intricately carved lattice work. All the bedrooms, seven on each side, open from within to access the verandah. Each room contains a large four-poster bed covered by a pristine white mosquito net suspended from a brass hook on the ceiling. These outer verandahs hold reclining armchairs, brass oil lamps, and a few brass spittoons.

The kitchens and domestic quarters are housed at the back, beyond the open courtyards. Behind the large kitchen is a vast open area known as the Maduwa. In days of the past, this would have been the liveliest section of the house. Here, in years gone by, one would have found women pounding grain in synchronisation over loud chatter and laughter, an occasional lewd remark cast upon an unsuspecting man who passed by. Delicious aromas would have drifted from the earthenware pots bubbling in the kitchen and assaulted the senses, mixed with the pungent fumes that emanated from the different spices laid out to dry in the blazing sun.

There were three features distinctive to this particular house.

The first was that it was constructed with materials that were sourced locally, teak wood, red clay, and black stone, although some of the original clay floors were, at a later time, replaced and transformed into highly polished cement ones.

The second feature of the house was the indoor ponds within the courtyards. These ponds collected rainwater from the open skies; the excess water was then drained out from under the clay floors, keeping the house cool.

The third feature was the most famous. Each of the open courtyards was flanked by eight large pillars. These sturdy columns were all panelled with ebony wood and, probably because of the abundance of ivory available from the ownership of the elephant kralls of old, embellished with decorative designs embedded in ivory.

These ivory embellished pillars together with the famous pairs of matching elephant tusks gave the mansion the title of 'Ath dhal walawe' or the Ivory Castle.

Chapter Three

"Castling"/Set the Pieces into Play

Agnes

eylon Daily News Birth Notice: Edward Solomon Wijenayake and Christine Samantha Wijenayake are overjoyed to announce the birth of their beloved daughter Agnes Elizabeth Kamalini, born December 18th, 1927.

It was at the height of British Colonial rule in Ceylon, a year after the birth of the Royal Princess Elizabeth, whose name was then bestowed on me, I was born into a well-respected, affluent, Sinhala Buddhist family in a Southern District of the Island.

I think the history of four generations that preceded my arrival needs to be related to really know me.

It is well documented that an ancestor of ours was a recipient of a title of honour and vast lands in the southern part of the island in return for services rendered to a local king. These same lands were later legitimised and gifted as a grant from a former Colonial Governor.

My great-great-grandfather who inherited, was said to have ruled these lands as an absolute uncrowned monarch. The villagers around cultivating the fields of rice and paying homage with the yields of their harvest. This very same ancestor was also remembered for setting up kralls of wild elephants, who he had tamed and then gifted to various temples to be used in peraheras.

It was in the next generation that my great-grandfather, a shrewd and far-thinking man, converted these lands into a commercial enterprise by turning them into large plantations of coconut. This contributed to building up a considerable family fortune. My great-grandfather was known to be a disciplinarian who governed these properties with strict rules and regulations. He was the ultimate authority on all social interaction, and every occasion needed his approval, every dispute was settled by him. Yet by today's standards, he lived a simple life, building himself a modest three-roomed bungalow in the year 1840.

It was my own grandfather, born six years later in that very same house, who cemented his standing in society by commissioning and building the famous mansion of today. This was done in the year 1870, just prior to his marriage to a noble lady of equal status who came from the neighbouring district.

There were some common factors peculiar to these esteemed gentlemen. The first was that they were all very dark and swarthy looking in appearance, and the second was that they sired just a single offspring. The second was an unusual feature in those times but it ensured that all their lands and fortune remained intact.

For many years after his grand nuptials, my grandfather had everything except for a son and heir. His noble wife had undergone countless miscarriages, and it was when they had all but lost hope, at the turn of a new century, at the cost of my dear grandmother's life, my own father was born.

My father grew up in the lap of luxury. The motherless boy was cosseted, petted, and indulged, but thankfully blessed with a sunny disposition and genial countenance, he was loved by all. At the age of seven, following tradition, my father was enrolled at his father's Alma mater and sent off to board at a private residence and attend a famous boys' school on the outskirts of the city of Colombo.

It may have been loneliness, or it may have been the conniving of a shrewd man from the neighbouring village, who sensed an opportunity and introduced his young and nubile daughter into my grandfather's life. Nine years after the demise of my grandmother, my grandfather broke with tradition and married for a second time. This young girl soon gave birth to a second son.

By all accounts, the stepmother, a simple village girl, had treated my father well, and in turn, my father, ever gracious, had been attached to his younger step-sibling. As the years passed and my grandfather aged, probably foreseeing problems arising in the future after his death, he bought a small estate nearer to his second wife's village, built a second house, and wrote it in her name.

The Ivory Mansion and all its vast plantations left intact, were bequeathed to his first-born son, my father.

Chapter Four

The White Knight/Edward Solomon Wijenayake

Agnes

My father, Edward Solomon Wijenayake, attended a prestigious school with the best of tutors, but as I learned later in life, he was not an academic high achiever. Yet, as a good sportsman, blessed with an amiable and friendly nature and a large generous allowance, he grew up to be the most popular member of his batch of classmates. He returned to his ancestral home during the vacations, but as the years sped by, it was apparent that he much preferred his life in the big city.

Once his school days were done, my father enrolled himself to follow various diverse courses of study to justify his continued presence in the capital. My wealthy grandfather was persuaded and proceeded to purchase a large bungalow in a prestigious part of the city, where my dear father resided supposedly continuing his higher education.

My father possessed a large group of friends and attracted many hangers-on, all of whom he entertained lavishly both at his residence and in the various clubs and restaurants he frequented. He was a welcome guest at most society gatherings and households and known to be a frequent visitor at the racetracks and casinos around town.

My astute grandfather, realising his son's lifestyle of extravagance did not bode well for the future, made a calculated decision and chose to introduce him to a charming young girl, the daughter of a dear friend. This young girl, my mother, came from a socially distinguished upper-caste family who was sadly financially impoverished.

My mother was the youngest of a family of three daughters, convent-educated and startlingly beautiful. It was an arranged union, and from the initial introduction, my father was instantly smitten. She herself may have had no choice and was compelled to marry to better her family fortune, but surprisingly, it proved to be a very successful union. My father adored her, and she reciprocated his feelings deeply.

The wedding which took place is still spoken of today with awe. The Ivory Mansion was renovated and refurbished for the occasion. The lavish spread of food laid out by famous caterers from Colombo, the decorations with the coloured light bulbs that lit up the surrounding gardens, the processions with elephants and dancers, the entertainment provided by a military brass band together with the attendance of many a distinguished guest, made this wedding memorable.

It was a match made in heaven as my father changed his errant ways and settled into a comfortable and routine lifestyle. The couple was blissfully happy together and affectionately referred to by their close friends as 'the beauty and the beast.'

Much to my grandfather's delight, his new daughter-in-law was not just a beauty but proved to be extremely astute and capable as well. She ran both my father's life and the household smoothly and in a couple of years she had taken over the administration and management of the lands and estates as well. I have heard from many outside sources that my dear grandfather trusted her judgement on all matters over his own beloved son.

I was born a year after their marriage and five years before my grandfather passed away.

Chapter Five

The White Queen/Agnes Elizabeth Kamalini

Agnes

I, Agnes Elizabeth Kamalini, grew up like the princess I was named after, wanting for nothing, loved and cosseted by all. It was not as if I was born with extremely fair skin, but having inherited genes from my maternal side, my skin tone was some shades lighter than my dark-skinned father, so from birth, I was not addressed by my given name but rather called 'Sudhu Baba', 'Sudhu Nona' or by my doting father as 'Sudhu Kumari', a white princess.

My life was a fairy tale. Blessed with loving parents, good health, and immense wealth, I lived a charmed life. My father adored me and refused me nothing but it was my mother who was the strength and glue that held us all together.

At the age of five, I was enrolled at a Christian convent school in the nearest town, to which I was ferried back and forth by our own buggy cart. The cart itself was fitted out with bright red rexine seats on either side, it had frilly lace curtains drawn across and had brass ornaments adorning the outer shafts. It was drawn by two white bulls with brass bells around their necks. I was always accompanied by my possessive ayah Soma who had been with me from the day I entered this world. It was her husband who drove the cart; their only son Siri, about five years senior to me, sat alongside his father and was dropped off at his village school, which was along the way to my convent.

I was twelve years old when the dark clouds descended, and my idyllic life came to an end.

My beloved mother, while out supervising the plucking of coconuts in a field a fair distance from the house, was caught unprepared in an unexpected downpour of rain. Later that night, she developed a high fever which compounded into a heavy chest cold, leading to pneumonia. Even with every type of medical intervention provided, she succumbed to her illness a few days later.

My father was devastated. Her sudden demise affected him most adversely. He descended into what would now be diagnosed as 'deep depression'. He kept to his room and took to the bottle, drinking heavily to forget and overcome his grief.

My mother's sisters had attended her funeral, and even at that young age, I had realised that my mother had never been close to her older siblings. Their relationship had been strained over time due to their constant appeals for money and their resentment at my mother's enhanced financial and elevated social status. When, a few months after my mother's funeral, I unexpectedly attained age, my maternal aunts descended upon our house once again. This time, after getting through all the time-tested rituals of isolation, bathing, dashing coconuts, and consulting astrologers, the aunts worked out a course of action to remove me far from this sad situation.

It was decided that I needed to be sent far away, so I was enrolled in one of the most prestigious girls' schools in the capital Colombo and packed off to their residential hostel. I had just turned thirteen.

It was a time of turmoil in my life and in the world. War drums were beating in lands far away. I grieved for my mother and missed my dear father and my home, but the move proved to be beneficial. The new experience of making friends and having company of my age and status helped me move on. I was not unhappy, and I enjoyed myself in the new school and settled in well.

When the vacations rolled by, I returned home. On my first vacation back, I found my father as reclusive as before. I was lonely and looked forward to going back to school and the company of my friends.

It was on the next vacation I noticed a change. This time I found my father's younger sibling—a constant presence in the house. My father also seemed to have many visitors around most evenings along with my uncle in attendance. These guests were lavishly entertained with alcoholic spirits and were not of the social standing my mother would have tolerated at Ath Dhal Walawe. Yet, since I was relieved to witness my father in better spirits, I did not think much of it at the time.

A year went by and it was when I returned for my next vacation I found an even bigger change. My uncle, aunt and their two young sons, around seven and five years at the time, had moved in and taken up residence at the Ivory Mansion. It was ostentatiously explained as being a temporary arrangement while some renovations were being carried out at their own residence.

Soma, my old ayah, was sceptical. I had to listen to a constant litany of complaints during that vacation.

Soma may have been right in her assessment and suspicion as the year passed, and it became clear that there seemed to be a sense of permanence in the situation. My aunt, a woman my mother had not been in favour of, seemed to have taken over the running of the household, and yet, since my father did not object, this, too, did not cause me much concern.

The very next vacation was the first time I crossed swords with my aunt. When I stepped into my home, I found out that Soma had been dismissed, and this irked me. I complained to my father and insisted on her return. My father, who could refuse me nothing, instructed my aunt to summon Soma and reinstate her back into service. It was at this moment of ill-feeling that I realised that I needed to take control.

I was sixteen years old, having just completed my first public examination. Like my father before me, I was not an academic achiever. Although I loved my school and knew I would miss my friends, I made the decision to quit school and move back to my ancestral home, Ath Dhal Walawe.

Chapter Six

Plan the Middle Game

Agnes

The initial adjustment was difficult, but as the months passed, I realised I had inherited my mother's ability to manage, and so I gradually took over the running of the household. I was greatly assisted by Soma and the older domestic staff, who favoured my presence back at Ath Dhal Walawe. My aunt was not pleased, but she knew I had my father's ear and that he would always support me. My orders preceded all others, so in time, I was acknowledged by all as 'the first lady of the house'.

In the subsequent year, it became clear that by registering my authority, I had upset all the plans and ambitions of my uncle and his wife. I was totally unaware that they had then resorted to their next move of removing my physical presence from Ath Dhal Walawe. They had now, supposedly, in good faith, appealed to my maternal aunts to look for a suitable partner as they felt it was the correct time to give me in marriage.

My eighteenth birthday was approaching. It was a time when the world was celebrating the end of the Great War, and my father planned to have a grand party to mark the milestone birthday. He had invited all his relatives and friends, my schoolmates were motoring down to join in the celebration, and although I was not keen on such a grand affair, it had been a while since I had seen my father so energetic and enthusiastic, so I did not fuss. I resigned myself to getting through this grand celebration being organised by him.

My outfit for that night was a saree and I was wearing one for the first time. The night before the event, when deciding on the accessories to wear with it, I asked my father to view my mother's jewellery. This was the first time I had done so, and while going through the valuable items, I remembered a particular ruby and emerald paddakama, which had been among the most favoured pieces of jewellery by my mother. This piece was not among the collection in the safe, but its absence registered, with my intention to ask my father about it. When the next night, I saw my aunt sporting that very same piece of jewellery, it provoked the final confrontation. I could not contain my anger as I asked in the presence of all my relatives why she was wearing my mother's necklace. She was totally taken aback, unprepared and embarrassed as she stuttered about borrowing the piece to wear at a relative's wedding. Since everyone was aware that this wedding had taken place a while back, it led to angry words and raised voices. This public confrontation led to my aunt and uncle flouncing off that night, and I finally succeeded in dislodging their presence from Ath Dhal Walawe.

I thought I had won the battle, but little did I realise that this was just a blip in their calculations. They redoubled their efforts to influence my maternal aunts to have me settled in matrimony.

Chapter Seven

Stalemate

Agnes

I t was six months after my eventful party and the exit of my aunt and uncle when my maternal aunts persuaded my father and arranged a formal meeting with a young man from Colombo who they considered to be a suitable match.

This young man was the only son of an eminent lawyer in the capital and his glamorous wife, a well-known figure in the social circles of Colombo. He had been educated at an elite private school and had just returned from Britain after gaining a degree from a university there.

I was, at that time, still very innocent and conditioned to believe that marriage was the accepted norm of what was expected of a well-bred young woman. Yet, as a strong-willed girl, I would have declined if I did not like the young man, but from the very first introduction, I was smitten.

From his initial gesture of presenting me with a posy of red roses, I was enamoured by his suave sophistication. He was confident, polished, articulate, and oozed charm. His worldly manner and amusing conversation captivated me. From that very first meeting, I was not averse to being courted and accepting him as a life partner. He seemed quite taken by my innocence and his parents with the substantial dowry I brought with me.

Although my father seemed reluctant to have an immediate wedding, his parents pushed for an early date, and since I was agreeable, the wedding date was set just six months away from the day we met.

It was the year before our little Island gained independence, a time for joyous celebrations, so my wedding was to be a very grand affair. It was to be held in a prestigious old hotel in Colombo. The gilt-edged invitations printed in London, flowers flown in from India, the best of champagne and cousine to be served. The guest list included all the elite of Colombo's high society.

Although it was my wedding and my father was paying for it all, the arrangements were being handled by my in-laws. I was driven to the capital for numerous fittings for my wedding attire and trousseau. My future mother-in-law and fiance preferred all things Western; I did not have any choice, nor did I venture any preference. My bridal dress was designed by the leading dressmaker of the time, and the diamond jewellery to match was ordered from a famous jeweller. Sadly, my mother's sarees and heirloom jewellery were deemed too old-fashioned and not stylish enough to be worn on such a grand occasion.

It was a new and novel experience of being the centre of attention in social circles. The excitement of the ceremony and the preparations preceding it overshadowed all the expectations I had of marriage itself.

I was young, innocent, and inexperienced in matters of love and sex, so I accepted marriage for what it was, rather than the 'happy ever after' fairy tale dream I had expected it to be.

In the first year of our marriage, we lived together with his parents. The year being the one in which the island gained independence and my father-in-law being highly connected to political figures of the time, it was a time of constant parties, receptions, and social events to attend.

Melvin, my husband, was not a bad person; he was just weak and immature. He, himself, may have been pressured into this lucrative union and not yet ready to settle down to a life of responsibility. Initially, in that first year, the novelty of having this simple, innocent and loaded wife who adored him appealed to his ego, but as the year passed, the novelty started to wear out.

Melvin loved the high life. Evenings out entertaining large groups of friends or being entertained in luxurious houses, clubs, and restaurants appealed to him. He loved all things foreign: liquor, clothes, and impressing foreign women at the various bars and nightclubs we frequented. I accompanied him but sat around, a demure wife in the background, not raising any objection as I knew no better.

The next year brought change. The renovations made to the house my father owned in Colombo and given to me as a part of my dowry were completed.

We moved away from his parents' watchful eyes to our own home. I was now occupied with the refurbishment and running of a large household. Most evenings, I preferred to remain at home rather than accompany Melvin around town. Melvin did not seem to mind.

I missed my simple life in the village, I missed my father, but Melvin rarely wished to leave the city, and it was a rare fleeting overnight stay a few times in the last year that I had been able to return to my home. Then, unexpectedly, my father fell ill. With his high consumption of liquor, his liver played up, and he was brought to Colombo to be hospitalised. When he was eventually discharged, I accompanied him back, and from that time onwards, my father's ill health gave me a reason to return to my hometown most weekends.

Melvin was known to have a roving eye. He admired women, most particularly foreign white-skinned women. The first inkling I had of his wayward behaviour was when a school friend of mine mentioned meeting him at a nightclub in the company of a young foreign girl while I was away out of town. When I confronted him about the incident, he brushed it off and said it was an old friend from his university days who was on the island on holiday. I believed him.

Although in the early days of our marriage, Melvin had not been in favour of my visits back to my hometown, he now seemed to be keen to send me off, seemingly very concerned about my father's deteriorating health.

It was about six months later, I was summoned urgently home as my father seemed to have taken a turn for the worse. Melvin professed to have some important work to attend to in the capital and said he was unable to accompany me.

That night, the doctor warned me of my father's serious condition, and I felt the need to inform Melvin of the situation. Telephone calls at the time were a tedious process, but after much delay, when I did get through to my house, it was only to be informed that Melvin was away that night at a seaside resort. I was furious.

Days later, when I returned and questioned him, Melvin explained it away as a 'spur of the moment decision' to get away with his friends because he was lonely. I was livid and, for the first time, made my views loud and clear, even mentioning the word divorce.

I think the altercation and rumours of Melvin's dalliance reached the ears of his parents, and fearing a scandal, they reined in their son and started pressuring him about starting a family in the hope of stabilising the strained relationship. It may have been Melvin's chastised behaviour in the subsequent months or all the prayers, offerings, and blessings invoked by his parents that a few months later, I found myself pregnant.

I had always hoped to be a mother but it was with mixed feelings I welcomed the news. On the one hand, I was happy; on the other, there was still a lingering uncertainty. My initial months of pregnancy were far from easy. I was terribly sick, and wanting the comfort of my father and the care of Soma, I decided to return to my home till I overcame the discomfort. Melvin, too, seemed to be relieved to be spared the worry of caring for a sick and moody wife.

The first month after my return home Melvin dutifully drove down every weekend to visit. He found life in the village dull and boring, and the next month, the visits dwindled to an occasional day trip. It was just after my first trimester that I got word that Melvin was due with a group of his friends on his way to the east coast on a hunting trip. This group of friends included a few of their wives and a young foreign girl who seemed very ill at ease in my presence. I did not give it much thought as I had to deal with a furore in the kitchen quarters, with a barrage of objections from Soma and the older domestics who all strongly believed in an old superstition of taking any life during my time of pregnancy bode no good for the family. Melvin did not give ear to any of their views and left a few hours later with the boisterous group, away on his hunting expedition.

Whoever knows what truth lies behind superstitions or beliefs, but one month after that expedition, tragedy struck.

Late one night we were awakened by an unexpected visit by my in-laws bearing the news of an accident. Melvin had been returning to Colombo from yet another weekend away, this time in the hill country when his vehicle was believed to have skidded off the road into a deep ravine. His parents were distraught, and although they did not mention a fatality in my presence, the fact that they had come to inform me about the incident made it clear that Melvin was presumed dead.

My father accompanied Melvin's parents and left very early the next morning to oversee the recovery of the vehicle and his body. My maternal aunts arrived later that day to escort me to Colombo and to make arrangements for the funeral.

The next morning, the 'Daily News' carried the tragic news of the accident. Melvin and his parents were well-known social figures in Colombo. The accident and his death were newsworthy in itself, but the subsequent discovery of a second body of a foreign girl blew the story into a sensational one. The woman had been thrown out and found some distance away, and as tragic as her end was, it was her identity that caused the sensation. The woman had been the very young daughter of a senior British aide to the recent Governor and a very influential figure at that time.

Although much money and influence were wielded to suppress the scandal, an enterprising journalist had unearthed the news of Melvin's stay with the young girl at a famous old hotel in the hill country.

Conjecture, speculation, and gossip about the relationship, the sightings at other venues surfaced, and I became the sorry third victim of this tragedy.

A week later, after the tiring days of the postmortem, the funeral, and the abundance of pity and platitudes or just the consequence of the old superstition, I miscarried.

Three months passed by, with me being in a state of listless lethargy. The loss of my husband did not affect me as deeply as the loss of the baby I had miscarried. My father and Soma remained with me in Colombo, but one day, Soma mentioned that she had heard that my uncle and aunt were once again frequent visitors to our home. It was then I decided it was time for me to relocate. I put up the house in Colombo for rent, packed up my possessions, and returned with my father and Soma to Ath Dhal Walawe.

Chapter Eight

Control the Centre

Agnes

The move back was smooth. I was happy to return to my home, but after a few months of doing nothing, I was bored. To occupy myself, I started taking an inventory of all the valuable items of antique furniture, crystal ornaments, and porcelain ware we possessed. It was while rifling through one such locked cupboard I came upon a pile of records and account books compiled by my mother over a decade ago. It meticulously recorded the monthly yields, payment receipts, and monthly income from the estate.

This awakened in me a great interest in the lands we owned. At the time of my mother's demise and my father's descent into depression and loss of interest in life, his brother, my uncle, had overseen the management of the estates and fields. As the years went by, my father had been happy to leave matters as they were. I had other ideas.

Like my mother before me, I started by inspecting the fields and storage barns and checking on yields. While questioning the labour, I felt that the yields and returns did not add up. It was then that I approached my father to look for someone with bookkeeping knowledge to employ. That was when Tuan entered my life.

Tuan Hameed was a handsome young Malay man from the area. His family was well known to my old ayah Soma. He was about five years my senior and had some accounting knowledge and experience. He was soft-spoken and very respectful, and I liked him on sight. Soon, he was a daily visitor with whom I went over the daily yield numbers and expected returns. After about four months into his employment, Tuan informed me that he suspected some pilferage, as there seemed to be a discrepancy in the numbers reported and recorded.

Some years ago I had succeeded in getting my uncle and aunt evicted from the residence, yet my uncle still continued to administer and retain the management of the estates. I approached my father armed with the figures in hand and conveyed my suspicions. When my uncle was summoned to the house for an explanation, he was furious. The resulting confrontation between my uncle and myself did not go well. Raised voices, insults, and threats towards me and Tuan resulted in my father ordering his brother to leave the premises.

Finally, I was now fully in control of the management of the household, the lands, and my inheritance, and like my mother before me, I revelled in the challenge. The task did not prove easy. My uncle had many on the estate in his paid service, and weeding them out proved to be arduous work. Yet, over time, I learned to be tough and shrewd, and eventually, the labour and the buyers came to respect my decisions and fear the consequences of earning my displeasure.

Throughout these transitional years, Tuan was my stalwart and trusted ally. He was never obtrusive and gave me the quiet strength and support to take over the management of my estate with confidence. From the very first introduction, I had been drawn to this soft-spoken young man. With the passing of time, I relied on his sound judgement, depended on his advice, and gradually started developing a deeper emotional attachment towards him. Yet Tuan was always respectful. He never encouraged any familiarity or crossed any boundaries to take advantage. He was a true gentleman.

It was a time in the country when we had mourned the passing of our first prime minister and were now moving on to celebrate the visit of the young Queen of England when my father, as a prominent figure from the south, received an invitation to participate in the felicitation event in the capital Colombo.

My father, being of frail health, needed assistance, and it was I who urged my father to ask Tuan to accompany him and assist him physically on the visit to the capital. Tuan proved to be an excellent carer. During the day, he accompanied my father to the official events and, in the evenings, proved to be exceptional company as he entertained him by playing chess or card games. I went to Colombo along with them and we all had an enjoyable time. I had never seen my father so relaxed since the passing of my mother, and this was when I started viewing Tuan in a different light.

It was also around this time that I started travelling further afield to view lands and small holdings we owned. My mother had purchased a few lands in her name in the neighbouring district of her birth. The political climate at the time was turning volatile, and the first stirrings of communal unrest had raised its head. Tuan had advised me to sell all the small holdings and consolidate them into one big asset, which would be easier to manage. These trips to view properties were day trips, in which Sirisena drove, and Tuan accompanied me.

It was on one such visit to view a property located further away that our relationship changed.

This particular journey was to be with an overnight stop as we had to conclude the business the next day.

We had made the booking at a beautiful rest house adjoining a stream of cool, clear water set in a remote area. That evening was cool and pleasant when Tuan and I dined together. Sirisena had retired to his quarters, and we were the only overnight guests residing there that night. After dinner, we parted ways to enter our respective bedrooms. We had been forewarned that the generator that supplied the power to the resthouse would be switched off at half past ten.

It was after I changed into my nightwear and settled into my bed and the lights turned off that I heard a strange thumping sound in my room. I switched on the bedside torch that had been provided and was confronted by an enormous toad hopping around near my bed. I leapt out with a torch in hand, ran to knock on Tuan's door, and summoned him to rid my room of the unwelcome intruder.

He, too, had changed into his night attire of a simple sarong and a sleeveless vest emphasising his chiselled body. With only the light provided by the torches we carried, Tuan tried to throw a plastic bowl over the toad, who was now hopping frantically around in fright. I myself was jumping around in my nightgown squealing with excitement. We were both in fits of laughter as Tuan finally managed to capture and evict the poor intruder from my room.

With this done, the atmosphere in the room changed. The air was charged with excitement, anticipation, and heightened emotion. Tuan closed the bedroom door and reached out for me. We fell into each other's arms in a tight embrace.

That magical night our relationship changed as we became lovers.

For all the following year we carried on our clandestine relationship in secret.

The nights spent out to conduct apparent business deals occurred more frequently. I then decided to use the money acquired by the sale of these smaller lands to acquire another property in the capital. The journeys into Colombo to view prospective deals took place often.

While in Colombo, we always stayed at my own matrimonial house. This was a large and sprawling bungalow. It was usually after we dined and I had dismissed the staff for the evenings, and they had retired to their quarters at the rear that we came together. We were very careful, but over time, the frequent sojourns alone in close proximity together gave rise to some speculation and gossip, which eventually reached the ears of my father and his family.

I had been aware that Tuan's parents had long been pressuring him to settle down, but it came as a great shock one morning when I was summoned by my father to inform me that Tuan would no longer be in our employment. He gave me no explanation or divulged the reason why his services were terminated; I did not ask, as in my heart, I knew the rumours had finally reached my father.

I never saw Tuan again, and he never contacted me, so I did not attempt to find him. A few days later, I heard from Soma that Tuan and his family had left the village overnight to relocate to the eastern coast of Trincomalee. Six months later, Sirisena let it slip that Tuan had married a distant cousin there.

I was heartbroken but I knew that Tuan and I had been in a relationship that was doomed to fail. The differences in our religions, social status, and wealth were obstacles too difficult to overcome.

Yet, to me, the time I had with him was the only time in my adult life I had been truly happy.

Chapter Nine

The Queen's Sacrifice

Agnes

The next year of my life was a sad and lonely phase. I missed the company of Tuan. With the whiff of scandal in the air, the news of Tuan's sudden dismissal had reached the ears of my maternal aunts. It was one year later, they paid my father a visit bringing along another proposal they considered extremely suitable for a woman in my situation.

At thirty years of age, there were many reasons I was not averse to entertaining the suggestion. Loneliness, the desire to get away from the endless gossip around my life, my father's ardent hope for a grandchild and Tuan's wedded state contributed to my decision to entertain the idea of a second venture into the state of matrimony.

Sudath Lionel Weerakody, as he was called, was a quiet, reserved man and at thirty-nine years, nine years my senior. He was an erudite professor of Literature at a prestigious university in New York. His commitment to his profession was the reason given for his as-yet single status. The fact that he resided in the United States was an added incentive as I was now ready for a complete change in my life.

Sudath seemed uncomfortable and awkward in his role as a suitor, yet that trait appealed to me. His elderly parents and one disabled older sister lived in Colombo and were simple, ordinary folk. Sudath wanted to have the registration done in a hurry as he needed to be back in the United States for his work and needed the paperwork so that my visa could be processed for me to travel over.

The wedding itself took place not too long after our first meeting. It was a quick, quiet civil registration with a handful of people in attendance, a far cry from the lavish ceremony of my first wedding with Melvin. We did not consummate the marriage after the official ceremony. Sudath was the total opposite of Melvin; he said we needed to give it time to get to know each other. He suggested we give ourselves a chance to develop feelings towards each other, and I greatly appreciated his concern.

He left the country a week after the ceremony with the understanding he would return in a few months, once my visa was processed and approved, to take me back with him.

I was ready to commence a new chapter of my life, far away from everything I had known and was familiar with.

A couple of months later, his parents informed me that Sudath was unable to return to accompany me back to the United States and that I would have to undertake the journey on my own. To me, who had never travelled anywhere on my own, this was a daunting task, yet when the visa came through, I was ready to undertake and set forth on this long journey by myself.

Although apprehensive about leaving my ailing father, the thought of new places to see and new beginnings excited me. After making arrangements to leave the care of my father, the Walawe, and the estates in the trusted hands of Sirisena, I set off to my new life with high expectations.

It was a long flight to London on a B.O.A.C aircraft, with stops in Bombay and Cairo, cities I never expected to see. I stayed in London for five glorious days with a schoolmate before boarding a T.W.A. flight to New York. I loved the experience of air travel, which was fortunate as I was destined to make many such trips in the future. I loved the feeling of independence, with the excitement of new pastures awaiting to be explored.

When I reached my destination I alighted the aircraft with mixed feelings of excitement and apprehension. It had been quite a while since I had seen Sudath. Our written communication had been stilted and formal, mostly containing instructions regarding the visa and flights.

Sudath was there at the airport to greet me, as proper and dapper as I remembered. He had a bouquet of flowers in his hand but he was not alone. He was accompanied by a younger man named Anton who he introduced as a colleague. The young man was noticeably ill at ease and hardly spoke a word on the journey back to my new abode. The conversation between Sudath and myself centred mostly on the weather at the time, details of my journey, and descriptions of the areas we drove through. Being newlywed and not having been in each other's company for a long period of time, I had not expected any demonstration of affection. Still, the lack of any emotion shown on that first day was perplexing and disconcerting.

When we reached his modest three-bedroomed house, I was shown to a neatly prepared guest room. Sudath professed that he needed to give me space to rest, adjust, and settle into my new life. I was quite surprised to find that the young man Anton resided in the same house. Sudath had never mentioned a boarder in any of his conversations with me.

Sudath never entered my bedroom, and in the first few days of recovering from jet lag, a change of time zones, and homesickness, I was greatly appreciative of his consideration.

Sudath and Anton left early in the morning to their campus and returned only around six in the evening. They had stocked the refrigerator with plenty of foodstuffs. We had early dinner together, usually a quick preparation by Anton when they returned after work. Afterwards, they both disappeared into their rooms to prepare for the following day's lectures as I was told. They did not expect me to wait on them, and I was usually left on my own, to entertain myself by watching television, reading, or listening to music.

It was nearly a week after I arrived, a time in which we had hardly spent any time alone to develop any close connection. I awoke very early one morning, and unable to sleep, I went downstairs to make myself a cup of tea. While returning to my room very quietly so as not to disturb the others, unexpectedly, Sudath's bedroom door opened, and I was confronted with a startled Anton exiting that room in only his boxer shorts and bolting sheepishly into the third bedroom.

I, who had been in two intense relationships, was far from the simple, innocent girl from a rural village as they may have expected. It did not take me a moment to understand the situation and realise the true nature of their relationship.

That morning I was shocked and shattered but I knew I could not bury my head in the sand. So that very evening over dinner, I confronted them together directly.

Unlike Melvin, Sudath was honest and upfront about everything. He did not make excuses or lie, and the truth spilt out.

Sudath was a homosexual man and in a long-standing relationship with his live-in partner Anton. He then admitted to the reason behind the hastily arranged marriage.

Sudath's parents and his disabled sister, although they appeared to be financially stable, were sorely dependent on his maternal grandmother to maintain their lifestyle. Most of their wealth stemmed from the value of the house and property they occupied in Colombo that was owned by his grandmother. Sudath had left home at a young age and, over the years, worked his way to be financially independent. On the demise of his grandmother two years ago, he had been faced with a calamity to deal with. His grandmother had bequeathed the very house and property in which his parents and sister resided to Sudath with one condition. He had to be married before his fortieth birthday, and failing to meet this requirement entailed that the property be passed on to a charitable institution.

His parents had begged him to comply as they would be left homeless and destitute if he did not marry by the age of forty.

I was once again the unwitting victim.

Chapter Ten

Moving Forward

Agnes

often wondered to myself why I did not leave Sudath and the United States at that time, but having undergone two stressful relationships with all the ensuing speculation and gossip, I was unwilling to return and once again be an object of pity. Away overseas, I was safely removed from the vicious and hateful wagging of idle tongues.

Another reason I did not contemplate returning to my motherland was the political uncertainty. That same year, the prime minister had been assassinated. There seemed to be turmoil and a general election to be held, and Sudath himself advised me against going back.

Sudath was a very good person. He and Anton took care of me well. I felt safe there, and I needed the time to figure out my future. So began the next chapter of the life destined for me.

It was a life of routine existence, which was in many ways suited to my needs at the time. I could not bring myself to reveal the true situation to my dear father, who still lived in the hope of a grandchild and the continuation of his lineage. I wrote back home professing to love my life in the United States but I hardly ever left the house there. With time, the seasons changing, and the sun out, I gradually started walking around, familiarising myself with my neighbourhood. I asked Sudath to enrol me in driving lessons and quietly ventured further away from home.

It was in one of those driving classes that I passed a real estate agency with a notice in the window advertising a vacancy for an office hand. I don't know what prompted me to walk in the very next day, but that decision changed my life.

The owner, Mr. Roussos, was an elderly Greek immigrant, a large bald man who, at first sight, seemed quite intimidating but turned out to be the gentlest of souls. For some unknown reason he liked me and I was hired. I was soon happily commuting daily to work. At first, it was a regular office job, answering the phone, making appointments, and dealing with mail and petty cash. Yet a year later, armed with a new driver's licence, I graduated to show properties to prospective buyers.

Mr. Roussos believed in me. He felt I had a natural aptitude for business, and soon, I lived up to his expectations of my potential by negotiating my very first big sale. It was not the money I earned but the sense of worth, with the independence it gave me, that I valued the most.

It was five years after I left the shores of my homeland that I returned. My homeland had been much in the news in electing the first female prime minister but I returned to a country undergoing hardship. Shortages of essential goods and talks of rationing were common topics of conversation, and although I was glad to spend time with my dear father, after a couple of months, I was actually quite relieved to get back to my life in the United States.

The next time I returned was when I got word that my father was in very poor health. This time, since it was going to be an indefinite period, much to Mr. Roussos's disappointment, I resigned from my job and flew back to be with my father.

A new prime minister was in office, the tide of Sinhalese nationalism was receding, private enterprise was being encouraged, and it seemed a more peaceful land I had returned to. I was glad I had come home to be with my father in the latter stages of his life. A little over a year after I had returned, at the turn of the decade, my father succumbed to his ailment and passed away.

I had been contemplating my future after the demise of my dear father. That decision was made for me when the former female prime minister regained power, and subjects of land reform and nationalisation became the common talk on the street.

With the passing of my father, I myself did not wish to deal with the forthcoming land issues, so with that in mind, I sold most of my lands, retaining just one residence in the capital and the ancestral Ath Dhal Walawe with its surrounding fifty acres of coconut land and set off back to the United States. It was also the time that an uprising among the youth of the country first took place, and was violently quelled by the authorities, which influenced my decision to leave. It was in the same year that the island officially became a republic and changed its name to Sri Lanka.

It had been many years since I had left, but soon after I returned, I paid a visit to my mentor and friend Mr. Roussos. This time the circumstances were very different. This time, I came as a client, and on his advice on properties that would appreciate in market value in the coming years, I was soon the proud owner of a large house in the prestigious Oyster Bay area of Long Island.

I left Sudath and Anton behind and moved on. I had long made my peace with Sudath. We both had acknowledged the fact we needed each other to get ahead in our lives. He provided security to his elderly parents and dependent sister and I found peace and stability in my mental state at the time. Over a decade had passed in my new homeland, and I was now confidently ready to face it by myself.

I spent the next few months happily refurbishing my new house and enjoying my independence. Sudath and Anton visited whenever they could to spend weekends in Long Island.

I spent a quiet, peaceful, routine life until one day, Mr. Roussos drove up to meet me, bringing with him a business proposal. He believed that property prices in Long Island were set to boom in the future and suggested I partner with him and open up a real estate agency here. This proposition interested and excited me. In truth, the routine existence had started to pale, and so I signed the agreements and was once again very busy setting up an office, building up new relationships, and completely occupied with this new venture we had set up.

In the next decade, I visited my homeland on a couple of occasions. It was after a landslide election victory of a political party, and terms like 'open economy' and 'free market' were bandied around. I enjoyed my visits back but did not remain on the island for long as I was fully committed to the business I had invested in back in the United States. I felt optimistic about the future of my homeland and hoped for better times ahead.

When I turned fifty-five, I started reaping the profits as the land values soared in Long Island. I was a millionaire and had become rich beyond my wildest expectations. I was happy in life, proud of my achievements but the one blessing that had passed me by was the joy of having a child to call my own.

It was on my fifty-fifth birthday that I decided to spend the harsh winter months away in the warmer climes of my motherland. My business was well established and run by capable staff. I had developed the early signs of osteoporosis and suffered joint pains when the weather turned cold. I felt now was the correct time to focus on religious and charitable causes, and so I started a period of travelling back and forth between the two countries I loved.

Soma, my maternal aunts, my aunt, and my uncle had all passed on. The two young boys, my cousins who had lived at Ath Dhal Walawe so many years ago, were middle-aged men and my only living relatives. Sirisena, my faithful employee, had remained a bachelor and was still the caretaker of my properties in my homeland.

Each passing year I returned, I found another calamity. Ethnic riots, civil war, and bombs were topics people dwelt upon. With the uncertain times, thoughts of death and succession often crossed my mind. My life may have continued in this set routine till the end of my days until the night the God above decided to fulfil my deepest desire.

It was in my sixtieth year, one stormy night when I found him seated motionless on the side of a lonely road. A little boy, my greatest blessing, my purpose in this life, a gift from God, and the love of my life. Motherhood, the greatest joy I had ever experienced, was granted to me when, on that fateful night, my son and heir Ashane entered my life.

Chapter Eleven

The White Pawn/Sirisena

Sirisena

I often wonder if her life would have taken a different path if I had kept my mouth shut and not reported the incident to my mother.

I often wish I had not.

I had heard much about the virtues of the Sudhu Baba long before I first saw her.

My mother had been hired as her ayah even before she entered this world. She lived in the Maha Gedara, away from me, her five-year-old son, and my father.

From the day she was born, my mother did not stop singing her praises. She held these virtues over my head, whenever she returned to our humble abode.

My father, too, was employed by the same household and was the custodian and driver of their family buggy cart. We lived in a small house close to the Walawe and for generations gone by, our very existence depended on the benevolence of this particular family.

On rare occasions, I glimpsed the 'little princess', as she was known, at a distance, but our paths did not cross until she turned five years old. That was the time she entered a convent school in the nearest town for her formal schooling. My father ferried her back and forth from that school in a buggy cart, and my mother chaperoned her on the journey.

The first indication of the changes in circumstances was the joy my usually taciturn father showed as his buggy was given a complete overhaul. It was painted white, fitted with shiny red seats and frilly white curtains, embellished with brass ornaments as it was readied and considered fit to carry forth a little princess. My father's pride and joy, the two bulls who pulled the cart, now sported leather collars containing shiny brass bells to announce her presence on the journey.

My village school was along the way and since my parents accompanied her, they had been permitted to drop me off there. My father sat ahead, and I sat alongside him.

Sudhu Nona, 'the white princess,' was not what I was expecting. I thought she would be proud and spoiled, but instead, she was a quiet, considerate, and caring little girl. Soon, like my mother, I was voicing her virtues and singing her praises everywhere.

I dropped out of school at the age of fifteen to look for work, and as expected, like my forefathers before me, I found employment in that very same household. I first served as an errand boy around the house, with my main task being to clean, oil, and light the lamps every evening, but a couple of months into my service, Loku Nona decided she would take me under her wing.

Thus started my training in the running and management of the surrounding land. I accompanied Loku Nona everywhere and helped with everything she wanted me to undertake. From counting the number of coconuts picked per day to marking trees that needed to be fertilised or felled to recognising the various pests to look out for, she imparted her solid knowledge and taught me everything. She was a firm but kind and gracious lady, and I worshipped the ground she walked on.

It was two years after I started working that disaster struck. My beloved Loku Nona passed on after a bout of unexpected illness, and like everyone else at Ath Dhal Walawe, I was devastated. It was as if the lifeblood of the house had been drained out, and overnight, this blessed place turned into one of gloom and darkness.

I was still employed at the Walawe, but I returned to my earlier mundane tasks as general help and errand boy. I missed my mentor very much.

It was early the next year that Sudhu Nona, as she was now called, left home to enter a prestigious school in the capital. My mother remained at Ath Dhal Walawe now as a general housekeeper. After Sudu Nona's departure, Loku Hamu's younger step-brother started to visit him frequently. In a couple of years, I had worked for Loku Nona, I had gathered that Loku Nona was not particularly fond of her in-laws. Yet at the time, like most others in the household, we felt that his brother's company may help lift up the spirits of Loku Hamu, who had fallen into a state of deep depression following the loss of his beloved wife.

A couple more months later, when Podi Hamu started bringing other men around with him in the evenings, the situation started to disturb the household staff. We knew these were not the type of people Loku Nona would have entertained, let alone tolerated at Ath Dhal Walawe if she was with us. Great quantities of liquor were consumed, and raucous laughter and loud card games with money exchanged took place most evenings.

I was the one usually assigned to serve and collect the glasses of liquor, and as such, I became a first-hand witness to the proceedings. Loku Hamu had started imbibing copious amounts of liquor and it seemed to me that it was greatly encouraged by his brother who always kept his glass refilled.

Yet, it was this very group of unsavoury people who brought about the change in my status within the domestic hierarchy. One night when the liquor stocks ran low, talk turned to an animated discussion on the benefits of owning a motor vehicle. It seemed to stem from the convenience of sending one out to procure more liquor from neighbouring bars and rest houses. A couple of months later, this came to pass. After much urging by his younger brother, Loku Hamu became the proud owner of a motor car.

This brought about a significant change in my life. Loku Hamu assigned me the task of taking charge of this possession and asked me to learn to drive it. 'Rosa', as I affectionately named, the motor car brought me great joy, and with much instruction and practice, I mastered the skill of driving and obtained my driver's licence.

The next year brought about another change at Ath Dhal Walawe. Podi Hamu, his wife, and two young sons moved into the house. It was conveyed to all as a temporary move while some renovations were being carried out at their own residence. This brought about other changes in the running of the household. The older domestic staff were retired or replaced. My mother survived the upheaval as when Sudhu Nona returned on vacation it was my mother she wanted and clung to. My mother was very suspicious of Podi Hamu's intentions and a vocal critic of his wife and her ability to run the household. This so-called temporary arrangement dragged on for the next two years, and everyone felt it seemed a very permanent move until Sudhu Nona turned sixteen and decided to quit school and return to reside at Ath Dhal Walawe.

It was evident from the outset that the relationship between Sudhu Nona and her aunt was not cordial. A few months back, at a time when Sudhu Nona was away in school, Podi Hamu's wife had dispensed with my mother's services for some perceived insolence. On her return for that vacation was the first time Sudhu Nona confronted her aunt and insisted on bringing back my mother to reside at the Walawe.

This strained relationship continued forward for the next couple of years when, on the night of Sudhu Nona's eighteenth birthday celebration, it came to a head. The final confrontation was the topic of gleeful conversation in the kitchen quarters as it brought about the departure of Podi Hamu and his family from Ath Dhal Walawe, and peace and tranquillity were once again restored.

This new phase did not last long as new changes were afoot. Six months after the eventful party, the late Loku Nona's sisters visited the Walawe, bringing with them a proposal of marriage to a young man they believed was extremely suitable for Sudhu Nona. They believed that at eighteen years of age, it was the right time for her to take the next step in her life.

The young man was the only son of an eminent lawyer and his socialite wife from the capital Colombo. After the initial meeting and mutual agreement, the auspicious day for the wedding was set. Sudhu Nona was not a girl to be coerced into any situation, but she herself was very taken up with the young suitor and was agreeable to take the next step into matrimony.

Surprisingly, my mother was not in favour of the union and the young man, but I was quite sure she would not consider anyone 'good enough' for her beloved Sudhu Nona.

I was just happy to see her happy as I ferried her along with my mother to Colombo for her bridal dress fittings and every other appointment in preparation for the grand celebration.

The wedding ceremony was the talk of the town both among the high society of Colombo and the village folk back home.

The following year after her wedding, we did not see Sudhu Nona much. She made a rare occasional visit back to see her father. She seemed happy, although somewhat subdued, which did not raise much concern at the time.

Drivers or chauffeurs of cars are usually the earliest to pick up signs of unusual behaviour or become aware when situations are brewing. They are the silent observers or recipients of unwitting remarks or gossip that takes place within the vehicles and it was in the next year I sensed all was not well with the newlyweds. Sudhu Nona was not the bubbly, carefree, confident girl she had been back home.

Since Sudhu Nona's wedding, Loku Hamu's health had started to decline. Over a year after her departure, he fell very sick and was hospitalised in the capital. After his discharge and return to his ancestral home, Sudhu Nona frequently required my services to ferry her back and forth from Colombo to visit her father.

She started by staying over during weekends, but as the months passed, her visits and periods of stay increased. By then, I had figured out that matters between the young couple were not all that rosy. She seemed happy to get away from Colombo and be back at Ath Dhal Walawe.

Then, one morning, we were all unexpectedly overjoyed with the news of the pregnancy and the impending arrival of what Loku Hamu so ardently desired, an heir. No one was more ecstatic than my own mother. She was deemed to have softened her previous reservations about the young husband. My mother was made happier when, a month into her pregnancy, Sudhu Nona's severe bouts of sickness made her relocate back to her childhood home and into the care of my mother.

The young husband initially drove down to visit during the weekends, but as the weeks went by, the visits to see his wife became fewer and further apart. One such rare visit with a group of his friends on the way to a hunting expedition made my mother apoplectic. Old beliefs and superstitions surfaced and were angrily voiced, to which the young man paid no heed and dismissed them as 'old wives' tales.'

Yet, nobody foresaw the future, and the subsequent accident and death of the young husband came as an absolute shock to us all. A day later, when the scandal broke, and the speculation and gossip that accompanied the tragic accident surfaced, we found it even more shocking.

It was with me, my mother and her maternal aunts we travelled to the capital after the devastating news. Sudhu Nona hardly spoke a word or shed a tear on that journey.

In the days that followed, we tried to shield her from the hurtful gossip and speculation around but to no avail, as it was the hot topic of conversation everywhere.

The stress, the travel, and the trauma of the funeral took its toll and proved to be disastrous. A week after the funeral, we all heard the disturbing news of the miscarriage.

My mother was devastated.

Under the doctor's orders, Sudhu Nona, Loku Hamu, and my mother remained in Colombo while I was instructed to return to the village and take care of the home front. It was after a couple of months had gone by after the accident that Podi Hamu started making an appearance at Ath Dhal Walawe once again. The visits grew more frequent as another month went by, and so, on a rare visit back to Colombo, I mentioned the occurrence and my disquiet to my mother.

I think my mother greatly influenced Sudhu Nona and Loku Hamu's decision to return. Four months after her husband passed away, Sudhu Nona, along with her father, returned to reside in the ancestral property of Ath Dhal Walawe.

After a time of grief and adjustment, Sudhu Nona settled back into the routine of running the household once again. After a while, she started showing interest in the lands and estates around. I usually drove her about as she inspected the fields and questioned the labour. As her interest in the management of these lands increased, she requested her father to hire someone from the area to help her reconcile the accounts.

I recommended Tuan, brought him into Ath Dhal Walawe, and introduced him to Sudhu Nonas's life.

Tuan Hameed was of my age; his family was known to mine as he lived near our house in the village. He was a quiet, pious young man who had followed a course in bookkeeping and was looking for employment. I liked Tuan, who was soft-spoken and well-mannered, and it was I who spoke to him regarding the job. It was on my recommendation that Loku Hamu recruited him into service to assist Sudhu Nona in her general household accounts.

Tuan proved to be an excellent employee and as the year passed Sudhu Nona started relying a great deal on Tuan. At first, I did not have much contact with him as his work was mostly confined to one room in the Walawe, which Sudhu Nona had converted into an office.

When Sudhu Nona had her uncle dismissed as the administrator of the estate and took to running the lands herself, it was Tuan who was her stalwart support. I saw her reliance on Tuan grow as she depended on him to advise her on all matters relating to the estates and other lands. She seemed to enjoy his quiet company. I often saw them chatting or laughing together and I was glad to see her happy once more after the tragic events of the past.

I witnessed their relationship progress from a professional to a more personal friendship, but it did not concern me, as Tuan was always respectful. A more peaceful, tranquil time was re-established and enjoyed once more at Ath Dhal Walawe.

It was when they travelled out further afield from the Walawe to inspect lands she owned a distance away and meet prospective buyers that their relationship may have become more intimate. Yet, I was blissfully unaware of that situation. Although it was I who drove them to these distant places, Tuan always kept his distance from Sudhu Nona. He was never familiar in his speech or actions, and I had absolutely no suspicion that their friendship had progressed into a physical relationship.

The trips into the capital increased in regularity. Her stays in her residence there lengthened in days, but it was after many months that on one of those trips I discovered by chance the true nature of their relationship.

Very late one night when we were staying overnight in Colombo, I developed an unbearable headache and found I was not carrying any medication to help ease the pain. I knew that Sudhu Nona would have some so ventured into the main house to ask her. It was well past midnight when I entered the main house to seek help. I was quite taken aback when at her room door I heard laughter and a male voice from within the bedroom.

It was the shock that made me refrain from knocking, but I did not return to my room. I remained hidden in the shadows, My throbbing head unheeded as curiosity got the better of me. It was at dawn when I was jolted awake from my sleep by the sound of a door being opened and closed. It was then I saw Tuan make his way quietly back to his room at the rear end of the house.

To this day, I often ponder if I should have held my tongue. I often regret having reported the occurrence to my mother on my return to the Walawe. It was she who conveyed the suspected nature of their relationship to Loku Hamu, which resulted in the sudden departure of Tuan from the residence and the subsequent departure of his family from the village which left Sudhu Nona heartbroken.

Ath Dhal Walawe was plunged once again into a time of gloom, upheaval, and uncertainty.

The gossip mongers with wagging tongues went into overdrive, primarily fuelled by Podi Hamu's wife. It probably was the reason that a year later, to everyone's surprise, Sudhu Nona accepted another proposal and, in time, after her visa came through, left Ath Dhal Walawe once again to travel to a far-off land.

Before she left the country, Sudhu Nona appointed me as the primary caretaker and manager of her father, home, and estates, elevating my role in the domestic hierarchy once again.

Loku Hamu hardly ventured out of his bedroom; he slipped back into a world of melancholy. He lived in hope for the day he would hear an announcement of the arrival of the next generation to carry forth the family name.

My life became one of regular routine, with me attending to matters of the house, labour, and lands.

Sudhu Nona first returned home nearly five years later. She returned to a country going through austerity and hardship. Other than being with her ailing father, she seemed to be glad to return to her life overseas. My mother and I both assumed she was happier there.

Her next visit back to her home was for an indefinite period of time as Loku Hamu's health was steadily deteriorating. She attended to all his medical needs, sat by his bedside every day, and gave him the comfort he needed until about a year later when he closed his eyes permanently.

Never in all the time she was back did Sudhu Nona get involved in matters regarding her estates or lands. She seemed satisfied with my management, but talks circulating around acquisitions and the 'land reform act' prompted her to put up most of the lands she had inherited for sale. She retained just the ancestral home Ath Dhal Walawe with the surrounding fifty acres of coconut plantation, one of her residences in the capital Colombo, before she left to return to her adopted country.

In the years that followed, we learned that Sudhu Nona had established a successful business overseas. I managed both the residences and the lands in Sri Lanka, as our island was now named. Finances were sent regularly, and Sudhu Nona provided everything I needed.

Sudhu Nona made an occasional short visit to Sri Lanka until she turned fifty-five and decided to change this pattern by returning to her motherland every year during the winter months in the United

States. This was a new beginning in her life, as she redirected her energy away from the business of amassing a fortune to being the pioneer of many charitable projects to help the disadvantaged back in the homeland.

I still drove her back and forth from Colombo to Ath Dhal Walawe on her visits back to the island. Life was once again peaceful and calm for her but not for the motherland, as ethnic riots, violence, and a war broke out across the country.

It was in the year 1987, the year Sudhu Nona was turning sixty that an unexpected detour on her return to the capital after the annual visit to her ancestral home, that the gods decided to intervene and bless her with the one thing she had desired all her life: a little child.

Sudhu Nona left a little over a year later with the little child. It was at the time of the second insurrection in the country, and in all the following years of turmoil and assassination of another president and other political leaders, she remained away, leaving me once again to oversee all her land and property.

PART TWO - BLACK

Chapter Twelve

The Opening Gambit

I t was past the midnight hour.

A lone spindly figure clothed in black, a frilled short skirt of red and yellow tied around his waist and similar-coloured frills around his ankles, pranced and swirled around an open blazing fire. A large fearsome devil's mask with protruding eyes and frightful sharp teeth covered the dancer's face.

The entire village had descended upon the clearing and were enthralled by the proceedings, fear and awe reflected upon their faces. The dancer occasionally pranced towards the audience and peered menacingly at a petrified spectator.

The heat from the open fire, the throbbing of the drums, the chanting of an unfamiliar dialect added to the charged atmosphere.

The tempo of the drums and the chanting quickened. The dancer went into a frenzy of twirling, tossing his head, and spinning around at an incredible speed. At the height of his frenzied spinning, he abruptly stopped and dropped flat on the ground. He pounded the earth with his closed fist upon a particular spot, where he proceeded to claw with his bare hands. Grass, earth, and stones were flung up as he continued to dig his way into the bare earth until, in one dramatic action, he arose, lifting up his arm into the sky, in his hand a small wrapped-up bundle.

The drumbeat and chanting ceased. There was a deathly silence as he gingerly unwrapped the cloth to reveal within, a blood-stained handkerchief, a tuft of black hair and a discoloured egg. In one quick motion, he flung them all into the blazing fire. The fire cackled loudly and spat out sparks and flints high up into the night sky at which point the Kathadiya fell to the ground in a dead faint.

The year was 1908. The Rate Mahattaya had been married over a decade and although over the years, he had sired many a bastard outside his marital bed, his wife Rosalin Kumarihami had not conceived and brought forth a son and heir to carry forward his illustrious name.

The Rate Mahattaya had been convinced that a Kodavina or evil charm had been cast upon his house and so summoned the Kathadiya to conduct a Hooniyan Kappana ceremony to cut the evil curse.

The Rate Mahattaya and his wife, dressed in pristine white attire, sat upon two chairs on an elevated platform facing the fire to view the proceedings. The heat of the fire and the crowd of villagers pressing down upon the scene saw beads of perspiration run down their faces, and at the height of the dramatic performance, caused Kumarihami Hamine to fall into a dead faint.

Upon her being revived and regaining consciousness, she was informed that the charm had been cut and the curse broken.

Be it the powers of the spirits evoked to ward off the evil curse, the power of the mind over matter, or just pure coincidence, six months after the ceremony Kumarihami Hamine conceived and carried forth to full-term a bonny baby boy.

Born early in the year 1910, the long-awaited son and heir Dullewe Mudiyansege Don Francis Hector Moonemalle made his appearance in this world.

Chapter Thirteen

The Ebony Castle/"Kaluwara Maligawa"

Five sturdy ebony trees loomed behind the large two-storied mansion that stood atop the hill. Twenty-four concrete steps led up from the road below to the front porch held aloft by imposing Greek-inspired Corinthians pillars. These pillars were adorned by elaborate mouldings of garlands of leaves and flowers. Every window and door was framed with intricately carved lattice work and enhanced with panels of coloured stained glass in brilliant jewelled hues. On either side of the imposing stairway of twenty-four steps were terraced flower beds holding a variety of multi-hued blossoms of flowering shrubs. The house itself, painted a soft pastel green, with its white mouldings and coloured stained glass panels, sat upon the hill like a multi-tiered structured wedding cake.

Through a heavily carved ebony front door, one walked into an open courtyard. A large fountain commissioned by a long-gone ancestor sat in the middle. The base of the fountain was tiled all around by a blue and white patterned porcelain tile imported from a far-off land. On either side of the courtyard ran two long verandahs. Old antique chairs with protruding armrests leant against the walls with gleaming copper pots holding indoor plants placed between the chairs. The sound of the running water from the fountain gave the place a cool and relaxed setting.

Beyond the courtyards on opposite ends lay two enormous reception halls. One was furnished with elaborately carved ebony couches upholstered in rich burgundy velvet and sat upon genuine Persian carpets that covered the floor. Crystal chandeliers hung down from the high ceilings and gilt mirrors and brass candelabra adorned the walls.

On the opposite end lay the formal dining hall. A long ebony table that could seat twenty sat upon another priceless genuine Persian carpet. Display cabinets stood at each corner of the room showcasing Waterford crystal decanters and glasses to hold every type of beverage. Sideboards laden with old English porcelain crockery and pure silver tureens stood on either side of the dining table.

The walls of this room were lined with imposing gilt-framed photographs of ancestors of old, dressed in the formal attire of those times who looked down upon the residents and guests of present as they dined in their hallowed premises.

An army of loyal domestics whose families had served this noble family for generations before were tasked with the tenuous work of keeping this mansion free of dust and cobwebs. A troupe of liveried males in pristine white coats embellished with polished brass buttons served the residents and their guests out of pure silver tureens.

Between the two large reception halls rose an imposing staircase possessing intricately carved ebony banisters. This stairway led up to the private boudoirs of this illustrious family.

At the very back of the house sat the enormous kitchens and domestic quarters.

The portraits and photographs of these long-gone ancestors reveal two distinct features. While the ones of the ladies and gentlemen of generations back are of fairer complexion and sharp patrician bone structure, a somewhat swarthier, darker-toned element seemed to have entered the bloodstream in more recent times.

For its famous location, set among a grove of sturdy ebony trees, its imposing ebony stairway, and its abundance of opulent ebony furniture within the premises, this residence was known to all around as the 'Kaluwara Maligawa' or The Ebony Castle.

Chapter Fourteen

The Black Knight/Kalu Kumaraya

allika peered out through the kitchen window. It was her usual and preferred spot in the room. A place she often occupied as she craned her head to gaze up at the big house sitting high above the hill.

The kitchen in this little house perched at the bottom of the hill was, as usual, a busy and bustling place. A place where Mallikas mother, grandmother, aunts, and neighbourhood women of the village gathered to gossip while making the traditional speciality sweets ordered by the owners of the big house on the hill.

"Kalu Kumaraya has finally been caught in the noose," cackled her old grandmother.

"The poor bride, I hope she knows what a sex machine she has captured," cackled another old woman amidst a burst of raucous laughter.

"I heard she is very beautiful and very, very proud," said Mallika's mother. "He must have finally decided to settle down."

"Settle down," cackled her old grandmother. "I don't give him a year, he will be back to his old ways soon enough."

Twelve-year-old Mallika soaked up all the gossip. Ever since she could remember, she had been fascinated by the lives of the residents of the Kaluwara Maligawa.

The present owner, Dullewe Mudiyansege Don Francis Hector Moonemalle, held her particular interest.

Kalu Kumaraya, as the present owner was referred to, was a reputed hell-raiser, womaniser and the hot topic of gossip on most days in that kitchen, but today he was the only topic.

Mallika had long suspected that her own grandmother had rendered sexual favours to a previous owner of Kaluwara Maligawa; it explained her intimate personal knowledge about the unusual sexual peccadilloes of that particular family. It was also common knowledge among the villagers below that the very same house they lived in at the bottom of the hill had been gifted to her great-grandmother from a former inhabitant of Kaluwara Maligawa for sexual favours rendered.

Here, in the kitchen, on the pretext of being keen to pick up culinary skills from her relatives, Mallika avidly followed the talk of the happenings at the house above. Lately, the kitchen gossip centred on this one topic: the upcoming nuptials of the present main occupant, "Kalu Kumaraya," as they addressed him behind his back to his future high caste, noble bride, hailing from the capital city of Colombo.

Mallika absorbed every word. The black prince occupied her every thought. She was fascinated by his colourful life and obsessed by his dark presence, which loomed high over her very existence.

Chapter Fifteen

The Black Queen/Mallika

Mallika

For as far back as I can remember, the Kaluwara Maligawa has dominated my life, and its inhabitants have consumed my every thought. I spend my days fantasising about the people who live there, and their lives fascinate me.

Kalu Kumaraya, the present owner, was my obsession.

The first tIme I actually saw him up close in person and came in direct contact with him was the same year as his long-awaited wedding. I was twelve years old.

My father, like his father and grandfather before him, were the village barbers and, as such, were summoned to the big house whenever their services were required.

It was a couple of days before the grand event when my father received the summons to report to the Maligawa. I pleaded with my father to take me with him to view the elaborate decorations at the premises we had all heard so much about.

After much deliberation and discussion, my mother and grandmother decided that I could be allowed to accompany my father there, taking with me an offering of a particular sweet-meat the Kalu Kumaraya was partial to, as a gift at our joy of his upcoming nuptials.

I recall that day well. I was bathed, powdered, and scented, my hair well-oiled and braided. I wore my best chintz frock with puffed sleeves gathered at the waist and long enough to cover my knees. I wore the only pair of shoes I possessed.

My father and I climbed up the many steps to reach the Maligawa. I was so excited I hardly felt the climb as I skipped up, even though I could hear my portly father huffing and puffing behind me.

Upon our arrival, we were directed to an open verandah at the rear end of the house. A single chair sat upon a large white sheet. A long table leaned against the wall; on it sat a white basin and a jug full of hot water. My father set about arranging his equipment of combs, scissors, razors, oils, soaps, and talcum powder neatly upon the table. I stood in a corner holding out my offering of sweets in a state of frenzied anticipation and then he arrived.

The first fact that registered upon me was that he was not as dark as his pet name suggested, and he did not possess the skin tone I had always been led to believe. He was a large olive-skinned man with a prominent nose, curly black hair, and a bushy moustache over moist, thick lips. He wore a pure white sleeveless banian exposing his muscular arms and a colourful batik sarong.

My father pushed me forward, apologising profusely for my presence and explaining that I had worried him to bring me along to view the decorations. He smiled, patted me on the head, and took one piece of the sweet-meat, biting heartily into its oily, sticky texture and smacking his thick lips. He reached into a purse tucked into a thick belt that held up the sarong and pulled out a coin. He placed it in my palm and bade me to 'run along'.

I was ecstatic. Fifty cents was a fortune to me at the time, but it was not the coin, the decorations, or the magnificent house that held my interest, it was the Kalu Kumaraya himself I had come there to see.

I skipped back home with my father after his work was done, clutching the fifty cents tightly in my hands.

"Achchi," I remarked upon entering our house," Kalu Kumaraya is not as black as you all say."

"No, Duwa, it is not the colour of their skin that gave them that name, it was always their dark deeds," answered my grandmother.

Chapter Sixteen

The Opening

Mallika

After the grand wedding, Kalu Kumaraya moved far away from my orbit. For the next two years, news of his doings trickled in through our neighbour and my father's closest friend and drinking buddy, Carolis Mama. Carolis Mama was employed as a chauffeur at the Kaluwara Maligawa. Little snippets of Kalu Kumarayas travels and details of his wife's grand residence in the capital city were occasionally relayed by him.

I, too, grew up, attained age, and became 'a big girl' as my grandmother informed me, and showed signs of developing breasts and a shapely figure. Carolis Mama possessed one son named Martin. He had been my childhood playmate, but he had now started pursuing me as a love interest. My interest in the opposite sex, too, began to manifest. My life would have probably pursued an ordinary and expected course if Kalu Kumaraya had not decided to relocate and take up residence in Kaluwara Maligawa once again.

This change of residence occurred due to his wife being pregnant. News of her ill health, her weak heart condition, and the doctor's orders of complete bed rest during the course of her confinement were common topics of conversation among the village grapevine. Kalu Kumaraya, his wife, and her mother, Lady Evangeline, moved into Kaluwara Maligawa with an entire entourage of helpers from the city.

This contingent of domestics from Colombo included the wife's old ayah Dayawathi, a regular battleaxe as described by Carolis Mama. These city dwellers looked down upon us village folk and did not encourage any interaction with them.

The son and heir of Kalu Kumaraya was born at the Maligawa two weeks before his due date. An eminent gynaecologist and a team of medical personnel were rushed in from the capital to attend to the delivery. We once again heard through Carolis Mama that it had been a difficult birth, one that had nearly cost the mistress her life, but thankfully, both mother and child had survived the delivery.

The birth of the little prince Siddhartha was rejoiced and celebrated with traditional food of milk rice and sweetmeats by us all at the bottom of the hill.

A month later, Kalu Kumaraya threw a lavish party to celebrate the arrival of his son and heir. It was held at the Maligawa as the lady of the house was too weak to travel back to Colombo. High society figures and celebrities descended upon our village. Fireworks lit up the night sky, a well-known musical band pounded out loud music, and liquor flowed. It was like the old times. Kalu Kumaraya was truly back.

In the next couple of years, the gossip and happenings at the Maligawa were widely discussed in our kitchen. The mistress of the house apparently had never recovered both mentally and physically from the ordeal of childbirth. Her heart condition had worsened. She suffered from postnatal depression. The doctors had advised complete rest, so the decision was made to remain in residence at Kaluwara Maligawa.

We heard from the kitchen grapevine of separate bedrooms with the dragon of the old ayah to get past to even visit the Madam. We heard of the staff from Colombo being constantly replaced, mostly due to friction, their inability to get along with the virago Dayawathi, and the sheer boredom of living away from the big city.

Rumours of Kalu Kumaraya's frequent and clandestine visits to nearby rest houses started to circulate. It seemed he had resumed his previous notorious lifestyle.

Chapter Seventeen

Capture a Knight

Mallika

At sixteen years of age, I myself was now well endowed and considered very shapely. I had Martin and many other young bucks from the village smitten; they followed me around whenever I set foot out of my home. Yet these callow youth did not interest me.

It was through Carolis Mama that we heard of a position for service opening up at the big house. The Madam and her mother were scouting around for a young girl to run after the little prince, who was now a toddler of two years.

After much discussion and deliberation among the adults, my father took me to Maligawa to apply for that role. Lady Evangeline and the old dragon Dayawathi were the ones I was taken to meet and who subsequently decided to hire me. It was a live-in position. My duties were to run behind the little toddler during the day, and at night, I slept on a mat in a nearby box room.

The first couple of months passed without much incident. The little boy was a sweet child, very much a mother's boy.

Every evening after his afternoon nap, bathed and dressed he was taken to his father's section of the house for an hour.

He was always accompanied by Dayawathi.

Kalu Kumaraya, as I had now realised, did not visit his wife in her bedroom. His dalliances with various women of ill repute were now open knowledge and a hot topic of gossip in the kitchen quarters. Other than a rare sighting at a distance, I myself had never crossed his path until about six months into my employment. One evening, Dayawathi, who had succumbed to a bout of influenza, could not accompany the little prince on his evening visit to his father, and I was instructed to take him there. This was when I came in direct contact with Kalu Kumaraya once again.

From the moment I entered with his son, I noticed that this time he looked at me in a different light. I saw his gaze lingering long on my breasts and buttocks as he looked me up and down and inquired who I was and what my work entailed. I noticed his eyes follow my every movement for the full hour I spent in his presence. I instinctively sensed the lust I had stirred up in his loins.

From the very next day, Kalu Kumaraya's movements changed. He started dropping into the child's playroom more often, and after a couple of weeks, he informed Dayawathi that since his son was showing interest in motor vehicles, he would be taking his son on drives in the car in the evenings. Since Dayawathi was known to be car sick on the surrounding windy roads, it was I who was delegated the task of accompanying his son on the evening drives. The accidental brushing of his hands against my bosom or buttocks, and the occasional pressing of his body against mine when handling his son all conveyed his interest, lust, and intention.

I was by now flattered and enamoured by Kalu Kumaraya. He had always been my obsession. I encouraged his familiarity and worked on enticing him with my body. I bent forward to let him get a glimpse of my breasts; I wriggled my buttocks when I walked ahead, tossed my hair, and giggled playfully. I knew full well he lusted after my body; I knew the benefits I could reap. One night, I felt his dark presence hovering over my mat as he stood over me for a while before he decided to retreat. I knew the inevitable would eventually happen so it was I who took the decision to take it further. I had just turned seventeen.

Late one night, when everyone around had retired to sleep, I bathed, powdered, and perfumed my body. I wore a long diaphanous nightgown that I had pilfered a while ago from the many that the Madam possessed. I unbound my long dark hair, walked across to his bedroom, and entered.

That night Kalu Kumaraya became mine. I satisfied his every need and for many nights after, these nocturnal couplings took place surreptitiously. He could not get enough of me.

It was not very much longer when my nightly visits to his room were noted, and tongues began to wag.

I had feared and expected the relationship to be discovered and reported. I had expected to be dismissed, and it had surprised me that it did not happen—until one morning, I discovered the reason.

One morning, I overheard Dayawathi and Lady Evangeline discussing the situation. The old dragon Dayawathi was heatedly entreating the lady to dispense with my services. She repeatedly referred to me as 'the whore', but it was Lady Evangeline's reasoning that it was better to have 'the whore' in the house where fewer people would be aware of it, rather than Kalu Kumaraya sporting his whores in public and causing scandal around town. So my nightly visits to his room continued unabated, but now my duties changed, I was no longer fit to serve the son; I was servicing the needs of the master instead.

I kept Kalu Kumaraya enraptured by my charms. He was besotted by my body and showered me with clothes, perfumes, and jewellery. It gradually dawned on me that his lust gave me power, and I was emboldened to aspire for more.

My first request was a simple one. I wanted a room of my own in his section of the house and close to his bedroom. He ordered a room to be specially prepared for me. He had it grandly furnished with every comfort provided. He heeded no protest or objection from anyone, and I realised the power I now wielded.

Kalu Kumaraya suffered from painful gout. I massaged his feet as well as his ego, and I took care of his sexual needs. He was completely in my power.

In time, my position as his mistress was established and common knowledge among the domestic staff, as well as the villagers below. My own parents and grandmother actively encouraged my efforts to keep the master happy; they knew of the benefits and rewards that it could yield.

Over the following years, I lived in luxury. My meals were served alongside his within his quarters. A young girl was assigned to me as a personal maid. Unlimited money for my use and a vehicle to travel around if I needed to venture out into the closest town.

Yet, to everyone else, I was a 'nobody'. I was looked upon and treated as a 'whore' by people who mattered. Most of the household staff regarded me in disgust, showing me no respect unless they were in his presence.

It was only within his quarters that I was queen; outside of it, I could not sit in public alongside him, but there was something in my charms that completely enraptured him. He never ventured out to seek new liaisons; he did not crave outside company. I was like a drug he was hooked on.

It was when the little prince turned five that I heard the first whispers of changes afoot. These rumours were usually carried up from the kitchen quarters and conveyed to me by my maid. It had been mentioned that the little boy was due to start his schooling in the capital. There was talk that the household was to relocate back to Colombo, and the Kaluwara Maligawa was to be indefinitely closed up.

I had gotten accustomed to a life of ease. My position and lifestyle were both threatened. I knew that if Kalu Kumaraya left this residence, I could be shunted out and regaled back to the bottom of the hill. When I confronted Kalu Kumaraya, he was apologetic, yet he explained that he needed to be in the capital to ensure his beloved son followed tradition and entered his Alma mater. His son came first.

He offered me a second residence in the nearby town. He promised to visit whenever he could, but I knew leaving Kaluwara Maligawa would inevitably change the position and the life I was accustomed to. I had no intention of letting that happen.

Chapter Eighteen

Plot the Next Move

Mallika

The random thought of 'what if' had occasionally crossed my mind, yet it had always been a fleeting thought; I never entertained the idea of an actual deed to make it a reality.

From the first day when I entered into employment at Kaluwara Maligawa, I had been made aware of Madam's poor health and seriously weak heart condition. It had always been the foremost topic of conversation in the backrooms of the domestic quarters. In my initial year of employment, I had often been in the room with her son as she lay exhausted in bed and saw the medication administered. In the recent past couple of years, I often wondered about what my position in life would be, if she succumbed to her ailment.

It was just one conversation, which I overheard, that pushed me over the edge and set off the madness in me. One morning, I heard Dayawathi speaking to all the other domestic staff, referring to me with the words, "Soon that cockroach will be chased back to the sewers she belongs in."

Months before, on a visit to a dispensary in the next town to collect some medication for Kalu Kumaraya, I had noticed that the pills in that bottle I collected were extremely similar in size and colour to the ones I had seen dispensed to the Madame. At the time, I had wondered if Kalu Kumaraya, too, had a heart problem. Madame was given that pill every night and as I was made to understand it was one that was essential to her survival.

That very afternoon, I chose to travel down to that same dispensary and purchase the same bottle of medication I had previously got for Kalu Kumaraya.

I bided my time till the next full moon day. The full moon Poya day was the only day of the month Dayawathi left the mistress and the house for a few hours to visit a temple nearby. That afternoon, after she departed, I slipped into Madam's room. She was fast asleep, as I had expected. I quietly tiptoed into the adjoining dressing room, where I knew her medication was stored. I was familiar with the bottles as I had been around these quarters in my early days of employment.

I took the bottle I wanted and emptied the pills into a small pouch I had carried. There were exactly seventy-seven pills as I counted. I replaced the exact same number of pills from the ones I had brought with me, wiped the bottle clean, and slipped out of the room without disturbing the Madame.

Not a soul saw me that afternoon; no one ever suspected my dastardly deed as I went about my daily life and bided my time.

I did not know what the outcome would be; I did not know if I would succeed in achieving my evil intention with my diabolical plan.

It was early one morning, exactly six weeks later, I heard the old dragon wailing. Soon after, with sirens blaring, Madam was rushed off by ambulance. Both Dayawathi and Kalu Kumaraya accompanied her to the nearest hospital.

In all the ensuing commotion, and when the coast was clear, I slipped back into Madam's room once more. I quickly emptied out that particular medicine bottle counted out the remaining number of tablets, replaced them with the exact number of the original medication, wiped the bottle clean, and slipped out.

Not a single person paid any attention to my movements that day. I burnt the tablets remaining in my possession in the privacy of my room and, later that evening, buried the lump of ashes in a far corner of the vast garden.

When the Madam succumbed to the diagnosis of sudden heart failure, there was no unwitting surprise. The funeral held was as grand as the wedding had been. The house was filled with mourners, with many prominent personalities attending. I had been ordered to remain within my room and specifically instructed by Lady Evangeline not to 'show my face'. Kalu Kumaraya was among the chief mourners there that day.

A month later everything changed. Lady Evangeline had insisted and persuaded Kalu Kumaraya that the motherless child was better served, removed from the tragic environment, and given to her care in the capital Colombo, where the little boy would eventually enter the prestigious school. The old dragon Dayawathi packed up Madam's and the young master's belongings and they all cleared out of Kaluwara Maligawa as I had hoped would be the result.

I was now the unofficial lady of the mansion, as I had always dreamed to be. I had just turned twenty.

I retained all the comforts I had been so afraid to lose, but my life did not go exactly as I had imagined or planned.

I took over the running of the household, although most of the staff left service and the premises, preferring unemployment to taking orders from me. I had difficulty in hiring new staff from the village, the few who took up employment came from areas outside the district. Kaluwara Maligawa was run by a skeleton staff.

Kalu Kumaraya himself was beset by many ailments. His mobility was impaired; he hardly ever moved out of his bedroom.

I was still his mistress but now more his glorified housekeeper and nurse.

Chapter Nineteen

A Diagonal Move

Kalu Kumaraya rarely left the Kaluwara Maligawa and travelled up to the capital to see his son. His son, as I was told, had been forbidden by his grandmother to set foot in the Maligawa while I was residing in it. Yet, although not close to his son physically, Kalu Kumaraya was inordinately proud of his son and heir.

As the years went by, and although I had every comfort I craved, life had become routine and boring. I was stuck at a young age with an ailing old man, and this was not the way I had planned to live my life.

My life changed the day Carolis Mama, whose eyesight was slowly fading, decided he needed to retire. He brought along his son Martin for an interview to be hired as a replacement. Martin, my childhood playmate, who had pursued me romantically in my early teenage years, had been employed away from the village in the city these last five years. I had not set my eyes on him for quite a while.

Martin was now a young man, broad, muscular, and virile. From the moment I set eyes on him, I desired him and knew it was meant to be. Kalu Kumaraya hired him as the replacement chauffeur. Before long and with no resistance, I seduced and enticed him into my bed. Martin became my lover and willing slave.

A decade flew by with Kalu Kumaraya providing my material needs and Martin satisfying my sexual needs, yet Kaluwara Maligawa itself was a gloomy and dusty abode. The few workers who were employed were unlike the ones of old. They had no loyalty to the family, no pride in their duties, and no respect for me. My Maligawa had fallen into a state of dilapidation and disrepair, much like its owner, who hardly stepped out of his bed. It was Martin and I who catered to all his physical needs. He was totally and utterly dependent on us.

I had heard from Kalu Kumaraya when his dear son proceeded to the United Kingdom to pursue his higher education, and upon his return to the island after he graduated I sensed a change in Kalu Kumaraya's demeanour.

It was when the son and heirs' twenty-first birthday approached, one morning, Kalu Kumaraya instructed Martin to bring in his lawyer to meet him at the Maligawa. It was Martin who eavesdropped on the discussion that ensued that day, it was he who relayed the distressing conversation back to me.

Kalu Kumaraya had instructed that Kaluwara Maligawa and his entire holdings and fortune be willed to his only son.

There was no official provision made for me in any form financially in his will.

It was as before: my position and existing way of life were once again under threat.

Chapter Twenty

Sicilian Defence

Mallika

Over these many years, I had never had any intention of mothering a child, but now my thinking and strategy changed. In my mid-thirties and with time running out, I needed to set this new plan of action, so I stopped taking the contraceptives I had religiously swallowed. With his ailing body and my sexual charms losing its appeal, I had to work hard to occasionally manage a few couplings, a benefit for which he seemed ever so grateful. Eventually, after much-forced effort, nearly eighteen months later, I conceived.

When the pregnancy was confirmed by the doctor, I set my next step of the plan into action and confronted Kalu Kumaraya. He was quite senile now and could hardly remember events of the previous day. I cried, cajoled, pleaded, and insisted

I wanted to have the child and needed the child to be legitimate but to no avail. Kalu Kumaraya was not swayed into taking that step. It was only when I packed up all my belongings and threatened to leave with Martin in tow that it finally registered that I was serious, and he capitulated. It was probably the fear of being abandoned rather than any feelings he had for me that he agreed to do as I wished. He was fully dependent on both of us.

The registration was done at Kaluwara Maligawa in secrecy. The local registrar was paid handsomely to keep his mouth shut. The reason for the registrar's presence at the Maligawa was inadvertently made public and relayed to all and sundry as the registration of Martin and myself. My own father and Martin's old father, Carolis Mama, were the only witnesses present. I had finally achieved what I had always craved to be, the legitimate wife of Kalu Kumaraya.

My subsequent pregnant state when it came to light did not cause much alarm and, although in my late thirties, was uneventful. Kalu Kumaraya himself hardly seemed to be aware or care about my condition or the situation. I had gained weight and, in the last month of my confinement, developed a severe backache. Needing some personal attention myself, I decided to return to my own home and the care of my mother until the time of delivery. I had every intention of returning triumphantly with my child to Kaluwara Maligawa.

Martin remained at the house to attend to Kalu Kumaraya and oversee the preparation of the grand room for the newborn, which I had ordered to be set up.

The best-laid plans can go awry, as the subsequent turn of events showed. A couple of weeks after I left Kaluwara Maligawa, Kalu Kumaraya's health took a turn for the worse, which compelled Martin to summon the local doctor. The doctor, on his return to the hospital, contacted Kalu Kumaraya's son to inform him about his father's serious condition.

That very evening, the young man arrived accompanied by two other burly gentlemen. Soon after, Kalu Kumaraya was removed by ambulance to the capital to be hospitalised. That very same night, with the help of the two gentlemen who had accompanied him, every room of the Kaluwara Maligawa was shuttered and securely padlocked.

Very early next morning, after bolting up the main house and leaving Martin in charge of the premises outside, the young master and his friends returned to Colombo.

My son, Mohan, was born two weeks later at the village hospital with Martin in attendance.

Kalu Kumaraya was never aware of the birth. He had suffered a severe stroke and was not conscious or mobile and remained confined in a hospital in Colombo.

I returned from the hospital with my son, back to where it all started, regaled down to the house at the bottom of the hill.

It was nearly a year later that Kalu Kumaraya finally returned to his home. He returned in a magnificent coffin to be buried with much pomp and ceremony at the ancestral burial ground next to his dear wife. The entire village and mourners from far and wide attended the funeral. The eldest son carried out all the rituals and customs, but the younger son and I were not in attendance.

In the days following the funeral, Martin conveyed the news that the young master had all my belongings burnt.

When I had left Maligawa, I had every intention of returning. I had left with just a simple gold chain and two gold bangles from the immense collection of jewellery I had accumulated over the years. I did not know what became of all the valuable possessions I owned.

Kaluwara Maligawa was once again shuttered and securely locked before the young man returned to Colombo.

Two weeks after the funeral accompanied by my elderly father and carrying my marriage certificate, I travelled to the nearby city of Kandy to consult a lawyer and stake a claim to the property. The lawyer was blunt and very clear.

He said a court battle would be a long drawn out and costly process. He also explained that it may be ruled against, as a willed inheritance would take precedence over a spouse. He also made it clear that in my situation I had little chance of succeeding and it would be wiser in everyone's interest to let the matter rest.

I was furious, but I knew I did not have the monetary means to proceed with a legal battle.

I returned home, disheartened and defeated.

My son, like myself, would have to grow up at the bottom of the hill.

Chapter Twenty-One

Ensure the King

Mallika

Years went by, it was a time I faced loss and hardship. My grandmother was long gone, Carolis Mama passed on, my own parents both were ailing, and my beloved Maligawa fell into rack and ruin; my life was at its lowest. The villagers shunned me, most of them very glad to see me brought down. Soon, my father succumbed to his illness, and my mother closed her eyes shortly after. I was left alone with my son, defeated and depressed. It was only because of Martin we did not starve. He was still my saviour, as I still possessed his absolute devotion.

The day a troupe of workmen descended upon Kaluwara Maligawa, there was great rejoicing in the village. We got word that the big house was to be opened, renovated, and refurbished. Then news filtered in through Martin that the young master was soon to be married and was planning to return and take up residence in Kaluwara Maligawa together with his bride.

My son had turned four when the young master and his wife eventually settled in. I heard the young man resembled his mother and the young bride was a lovely young lass from the neighbouring city of Kandy. She hailed from a good family and unlike the former Madam who had been known for her arrogance, was a simple and gentle girl. This young couple was soon adored by everyone in the village below.

The legislation introduced years before had significantly reduced the extent of land owned by the family, but the young master was determined to develop the acres he had inherited. He was intent on lifting up the lives of the villagers around him and believed to have political ambitions. He was known to be generous and helpful to everyone, but probably influenced by his grandmother and old Dayawathi, he shunned me. I was never a recipient of any handout.

Martin continued to work as a driver at Kaluwara Maligawa, and it was through him that I learned of the happenings at the big house above. The fascination I had harboured from my childhood with the lives lived within the Maligawa had not dimmed.

The pregnancy and the birth of their son were all relayed to me, and the grand celebrations that followed to mark the occasion were described in detail and absorbed by me with avid interest.

I had resigned myself to my diminished status in life and life may have continued in this vein if that one incident had not occurred to awaken the madness in me once again.

Although initially, in my relationship with Kalu Kumaraya, I never had an intention to birth a child, when my son was born, my feelings underwent a dramatic change. From the day I first held him in my arms at the village hospital, he was my life. At that time of turmoil and trouble, when I fell into deep depression he was the reason I held on. He was my saviour; having him kept me sane.

It happened one night some months after the young master became a father himself. It happened on a night Martin was away with the young family in the capital. Late one night, my own dear young son fell seriously ill. He was running a temperature so high, his body seemed to be on fire. I was alone, frightened and desperate. When he started having convulsions I panicked. I ran up the steps to Kaluwara Maligawa, I had never ventured up there since the day I had left many years back. It may have been instructions given to never entertain my presence; it may have been cussedness on the part of the domestic staff or just plain disregard and disdain for the needs of the less fortunate, nobody gave a hearing to my pleas for help. They chased me out as they would a stray dog, hurling hateful abuse.

I returned defeated, and although my son survived that night, I could not get over the humiliation. It awoke in me the devil I thought I had subdued. It was that humiliation that hardened my resolve to get even, to change the acceptance of my situation. It was on that night, crying over my sick young son that the dark thoughts of 'what if' entered my head.

From childhood, Martin had been my playmate, from those childhood games which he wilfully let me win, to being his teenage crush where I had ridiculed his affection, my besotted lover and the current breadwinner, he was and always had been my slave.

Now, when I fantasised about the future, playing out various scenarios in my twisted mind, he indulged me by listening. It was only to Martin I articulated my deadly intentions.

Martin resisted entertaining any such thoughts, but I worked on his emotions, breaking down all opposition he voiced on my diabolical plans. I always believed that when the opportunity arose I could get Martin to do as I bid. I envisaged many a dastardly scheme and imagined many possible scenarios, but it was all in my head; I never had any opportunity to carry out any plan that I had thought of. My path never crossed the young master, the present owner of Kaluwara Maligawa, or his family.

The opportunity, as I was convinced would work arose sometime much later. It was when Martin mentioned a particular occasion being held at a particular location that he would be taking the young family to attend some months ahead that a dark plan sprang into my mind and took root.

Persuading Martin proved to be more difficult, yet eventually, with pleas, tears, withholding favours, promises, and finally threats of self-harm, he finally capitulated and agreed to carry out my deadly plan.

It was the only way to once again ascend that hill and return triumphantly to reign once again as the mistress of Kaluwara Maligawa.

Chapter Twenty-Two

The Black Pawn/Martin

Martin

Mallika was mine. From the day she was placed in my six-year-old arms, opened her almond-shaped black eyes, and smiled up at me, I was possessed; I considered her my own.

Our fathers were good friends and drinking buddies. We lived in neighbouring houses in the shadows of a big mansion. Kaluwara Maligawa loomed high above our humble abodes and influenced every aspect of our lives.

My father was employed as a chauffeur by the Loku Hamu of the Maligawa and her father was the local village barber.

Mallika and I grew up at the bottom of the hill and were inseparable as childhood playmates.

Although I was older, she was always the dominant one. I indulged her demands, abided by her rules, went along with her every whim, carried out her bidding, and let her win in all the games we played. She commanded, and I obeyed.

Yet, although I was totally possessed by her, her obsession lay elsewhere. She was obsessed with the Kaluwara Maligawa and all who resided within. She spent hours gazing up at the mansion visible from the kitchen window below. She hung on every word my father spouted about the owner who now occupied it and everything that took place within. As children and at her insistence, we spent many an afternoon roaming around the vast gardens, most often chased away by the gardeners working there.

The Loku Hamu to whom the Maligawa belonged did not occupy the house. He preferred life in the capital city of Colombo. He was famous throughout the district for his extravagant lifestyle and his infamous liaisons with numerous women. This notoriety earned him the title Kalu Kumaraya, a name by which he was commonly referred to, by all the villagers.

The Maligawa was usually desolate and deserted, but on his rare visits back to the residence, the atmosphere changed. He was always accompanied by a large group of boisterous friends. Lights blazed out throughout the night, and loud music blared out with total disregard for disturbing the peace and tranquillity of the surrounding area. Food was cooked in abundance and liquor overflowed. Most of the villagers below were employed in various tasks to feed or entertain the guests. Foreign women in skimpy swimwear were seen frolicking in the streams around. Picnics and hikes were organised to view the picturesque landscape around. His visits back turned the usual sleepy hamlet into a scandalous festive one.

Although, as children, we were not directly involved with the shenanigans, the excitement and gossip around the happenings kept us entertained for months after. Kalu Kumaraya's dalliances with well-known socialite ladies and some other notoriously infamous ones were intensely discussed and dissected, most of this gossip directly imparted by my father, who drove him around. From a very young age, Mallika was the most avid follower of the information relayed.

The impending change to his marital status took us all by surprise. Kalu Kumaraya was already in his mid-forties, and most of us had believed he would remain a bachelor for life; the news of his upcoming nuptials to be held at Kaluwara Maligawa came as a welcome distraction to our mundane existence and the excitement in the village grew to a fever pitch.

The lady to whom he was betrothed, hailed from the high social circle of Colombo and was said to be extremely beautiful. When she finally arrived at Kaluwara Maligawa, news filtered down that she was very proud and arrogant and regarded our part of the world as 'backward'.

Mallika was enthralled by it all, and to her great joy, a couple of days before the big event, she was permitted to accompany her father to the Maligawa. It was the first time she had actually been inside the mansion, and although she was fascinated by the interior, from that fateful day, she seemed not only to be obsessed with the Maligawa but also possessed by Kalu Kumaraya himself.

After the lavish wedding ceremony and the couple and guests' departure, the village returned to its sleepy state and we went on with our routine life. The only time of excitement occurred was when Mallika was held in isolation and emerged a week later decked out in new attire and gold earrings and I was made aware of her 'big girl' status.

This was when my interest in her progressed from friendship into desire. I was nineteen, and she was just thirteen, but even at that young age, she understood the power she wielded over me. I followed her around the village, picking fights with any other village lad who glanced her way, yet most often, they were not to blame as she encouraged and enticed them to fuel my jealousy.

Life continued in a slow-paced vein; I was looking around for suitable employment at the time. Occasional snippets of the doings of Kalu Kumaraya filtered in through my father when, one day, we got word that there was renewed activity at Kaluwara Maligawa. The mansion had been reopened, renovations with modern bathrooms and kitchens were being installed, and we got the good news of the impending arrival of the couple and the happy news of the impending arrival of the heir. The lady had been advised of complete bed rest due to her severe sickness, and she had decided to spend her confinement in the cooler climes of our part of the island, so Kalu Kumaraya and his wife relocated back to Kaluwara Maligawa.

The villagers at the bottom of the hill were all agog with excitement and anticipation but when the young Madam eventually came into the residence, she came with her own retinue of domestics. Heading them all was a formidable older woman called Dayawathi who we heard had been the ayah to the present Madam when she was a baby.

The Maligawa was no longer a bastion for the old guard who had served the family for generations. A new guard had moved in, and the village folk were no longer tolerated above.

Yet, my father retained his post as the household driver, and it was through him, details of the difficult confinement and eventual near-fatal delivery reached the local grapevine.

It was after the excitement of hearing of the birth of the next generation, the son and heir Siddhartha that the Madam's serious health condition, her continued confinement in her room and bed became common topics of conversation among the villagers.

Among the more lurid gossip was the reluctance of the old ayah to let anyone visit the young Madam including her own husband Kalu Kumaraya.

The master still resided at Kaluwara Maligawa, but soon, talk of his visits to neighbouring rest houses with ladies of questionable reputations surfaced. My father was a first-hand witness to all the notorious activities.

When the little prince turned two, my life changed course. I had always believed that I would be married to Mallika as soon as she was old enough. I never imagined she would choose to pave her own way in life, so when she opted to take up a live-in position as a nursery maid, it came as a great shock to me. She was sixteen years old at the time. I did not see her after she left to take up employment, and although it was a difficult period in my life, it was not as devastating as when, a year later, the rumours of her relationship with Kalu Kumaraya started circulating around.

My father and hers both realised my distress and despair, but they both understood the benefits she could reap. So, encouraged by the elders of both families, I left the village to take up employment in the nearby town of Kandy.

I hardly ever returned to the village; on the very rare occasion I did, it was to hear more gossip about her now confirmed and scandalous position as the mistress of Kalu Kumaraya.

I myself considered handsome and eligible in the village, could never form any serious relationships as, although I did not attempt to see her, my obsession for Mallika never waned.

I eventually returned home to stay permanently at my father's bidding. My mother was on her deathbed, my father's eyesight failing, and as a dutiful son, I acceded to his wish. My father had already spoken to Kalu Kumaraya and lined me up to be employed as his replacement.

I was thirty years old when I reported to the Maligawa to take up my duties and saw Mallika once again. Gone was that innocent comely young girl with her long hair braided into two long plaits. She stood alongside Kalu Kumaraya, transformed into this voluptuous, enticing, bold siren. Her hair fell loose, she looked me up and down with her large hooded eyes, her hips thrust out, her luscious lips coloured, her innocence long gone. Here stood before me a woman who was fully aware of her charms and the power she possessed over men. I was bewitched and enamoured once more.

It was only a couple of days later, she requested the car at her disposal to visit the nearest town. It was on her journey back she ordered me to visit her quarters that night. She made it obviously clear that she desired my body and I had no power or will to resist.

I clocked out that evening as usual but instead of dismounting the steps to my house below, I slipped unnoticed into her room. She was waiting for me and took me by the hand and led me to her bed. This was what I had forever desired. I became a slave to all her wants and needs as I fell under her spell once more.

My life changed with her re-entry into my life. It was dominated by her dark presence. Our clandestine trysts continued unabated and often. She was insatiable. Although the staff at Kaluwara Maligawa had depleted considerably, there were still a few milling around, and the need to be discreet was always on my mind. Yet as time passed and our couplings got bolder, it probably reached the ears of Kalu Kumaraya, but he chose to turn a blind eye. He was by now a lonely, sick man, and he needed Mallika more than ever and seemed totally dependent on her. Mallika used this to her advantage and procured a room for me at the Maligawa and I soon became a resident within.

We lived in comfort. Mallika controlled his body and his purse. He dispensed money whenever she wanted and she had full authority over the running of the household.

As the years rolled by, Kalu Kumaraya rarely ventured outside the Maligawa; in fact, he hardly ever left his room. His only son never set foot in the Maligawa to visit.

The day I was asked to transport his lawyer to meet him at the house was the day the son turned twenty-one. I was curious about the unexpected visit, so I listened to their conversation. It was then that I overheard Kalu Kumaraya dictate his last will and testament, leaving Kaluwara Maligawa and everything else he possessed to his beloved son.

Mallika was furious when I conveyed the information. She was not one to accept any threat to her rule at Kaluwara Maligawa. It was soon clear to me that she was thinking far ahead and plotting her next move.

It was eighteen months later; her scheme bore results with her conceiving a child.

The subsequent coerced secret registration of Kalu Kumaraya was plotted and arranged through her father and mine, and conveyed to the village below, that Mallika and I were, at long last, man and wife.

It was the severe back pain she suffered that made her decide to leave Maligawa and reside with her mother in the last stages of her pregnancy. I remained in the big house to take care of Kalu Kumaraya and oversee the preparation of the grand nursery for the soon-expected unborn child. Mallika had every intention of returning to Kaluwara Maligawa with her baby in triumph.

One can never foresee what lies ahead, and we never anticipated the events that followed to thwart Mallika's well-set scheme. One morning, I found Kalu Kumaraya very ill. He seemed disoriented and rambling incoherently, and I was compelled to summon the local doctor to attend to him. The young man who arrived suspected the onset of a stroke and subsequently, unbeknownst to me, had directly informed his son in Colombo.

It came as a surprise to me that very evening when Kalu Kumaraya's son, accompanied by two hefty gentlemen, arrived at Kaluwara Maligawa. An ambulance followed, by which the master was immediately transferred to the capital, Colombo, for treatment.

The son remained with his companions and, that very same night, proceeded to shutter and padlock every room in the mansion. Early the next morning, after securely locking up the main house, they left me in charge of maintaining the premises outside and returned to Colombo.

Mallika's son, presumed by all at the village to be mine, was born a fortnight later in the village hospital. She named him Mohan. Soon after, she withdrew into her own world, and it was only this child that kept her living.

It was nearly a year later Kalu Kumaraya returned home to Kaluwara Maligawa. He was brought back to be laid to rest with much pomp and pageantry in the family burial ground. Mallika and her son were notable absentees.

It was a week after the funeral, I saw the Mallika of old. She had roused herself from her stupor to fight her cause. A few days later accompanied by her father, she travelled up to the city of Kandy to consult a lawyer regarding her status and rights. It was an enraged Mallika who returned, as the lawyer had advised against initiating legal recourse and contesting the will.

There was one characteristic trait that I was sure about in Mallika: from her early childhood, she did not like to lose. She spent hours contemplating her next move and many a day, I would find her gazing up through the kitchen window at Kaluwara Maligawa.

For over another couple of years, Kaluwara Maligawa was kept securely locked. The house looked neglected and was falling into disrepair till one morning, a troupe of workmen descended upon the big house to carry out extensive renovations.

The news spread fast and there was great rejoicing in the village with word of the young master's marriage to a young lass from the neighbouring city of Kandy and his intention to move back into the Maligawa with his new bride.

When the young master and his wife eventually moved in, I found the master quite unlike Kalu Kumaraya both in appearance and character. He was devoted to his young wife and genuinely keen on helping the villagers below uplift their lives. We heard he had political ambition. His young wife, too, was unlike the previous Madam. She was kind and simple, and soon, everyone rejoiced at their return and presence at Kaluwara Maligawa.

Mallika, who had still not come to terms with her degraded status was the only person seething with resentment.

I continued to hold my position and be employed as the driver and remained the sole breadwinner for Mallika and her son.

A year later, the village had reason to rejoice once more as a grand celebration heralded the arrival of the next generation with the birth of the son and heir, Rahula Nissanka Moonemalle.

I was happy with the present situation. Life was routine and peaceful. In fact, over time, I felt Mallika, too, seemed resigned to her fate in life. I believed her obsession with the Maligawa had waned. This mundane existence may have continued unabated if that one single incident that occurred, had not set off a wicked train of thought and brought on the streak of madness she possessed. It revived Mallika's sleeping desire for vengeance and rekindled her obsession with holding absolute power and being the mistress of Kaluwara Maligawa once again.

The said incident occurred at a time when I was away from the village having driven with the master and his family to Colombo. It had been late one night when Mohan, her young son had developed a very high fever. It was when he had started convulsions that a panicked Mallika had in desperation run up to the Walawe to seek help in getting the boy to the nearest medical centre. It may have been that the staff were following instructions, or they were just plain unsympathetic and indifferent to her plight that they did not give her any heed, but it was the abuse hurled and the ridicule she encountered that rankled and hurt as she was chased out that night.

It was then the determination to get even with the very people who shunned her that started off the dark train of thoughts and sent her on a path of madness to exact revenge and retribution. I returned to a woman who was ranting and raving over the injustices she had been subjected to. At times, she seemed unhinged as she started voicing many a dastardly plan or scenario in which she could achieve her goal. I humoured her by listening to what I assumed were her imaginary fantasies and believed these would only play out in her twisted mind. I thought over time, she would tire of this exercise; little did I know she was deadly serious.

If I had only taken her insanity seriously, I would never have divulged any details on the life or upcoming plans of the young family, but one day, I mentioned a particular event the family would be attending in a couple of months. It was to a family wedding outstation and it was this location of the wedding venue that Mallika became fixated upon. This was a place high in the hill country known for its treacherous bends, narrow roads, and numerous accidents.

Days later, she pictured and presented very clearly her dastardly plan. I was at first sceptical, then unwilling, and finally terrified, but Malika did not back down. With tears, persuasion and threats she wore out my opposition, till finally I capitulated.

I had always been weak when it came to Mallika, and she was well aware of it.

A month later, I set off with the young master and his family on that fateful journey upcountry. It was a long drive when we arrived at the picturesque resthouse, where they changed into their finery before leaving for the function. They were due back later to stay overnight. I drove them to the venue that evening. It was a slow journey as there was an incessant drizzle, and the narrow roads were wet and slippery. It was around six thirty that evening when we reached the venue, and the family dismounted, and I drove the vehicle away to a secluded spot to park. It was here, away from any watchful eyes, that I severed a part of the brake lining.

After completing the first part of this despicable mission, I left the car in the parking lot and returned to the venue on foot. Here, I sent an urgent message to the young master that I needed to speak to him.

I was, at this point, literally shaking in fear, so when I told the young master that I was feeling too ill to drive, I actually felt sick and nauseous. The good man that he was, handed me some money and requested me to get back to the village as he himself could drive his family back after the celebrations. It was around eight that night when I handed him the car keys and left. This interaction was witnessed by several of the guests at the venue.

The next part of the plan had been plotted and arranged a week back. Here, Mallika had hired and arranged for a lorry to be parked at a designated spot close by. I travelled by foot unseen to where the lorry was parked upon an incline and hidden from view. The keys were hidden within as requested.

I climbed up into this lorry from where I could witness all the vehicles exiting the car park. To add to my intention of being unseen, the drizzle had increased into a steady downpour.

I was on edge, extremely nervous, as I sat waiting anxiously and partook of more than a few swigs of the local alcoholic beverage to bolster up my nerves.

It was just past ten that night when I saw the master's car pull out of the car park and hit the main road. I drove down the incline and followed the car at a distance but always keeping it in sight. The young master, probably unfamiliar with these narrow, wet roads, drove at a snail's pace as I crawled behind.

Nearly half an hour later, we reached the infamous treacherous bends. The rain was pelting down, making visibility near impossible. There were no other vehicles in sight when I increased my speed to tail the car. At a steep, sharp bend on the narrow road, I accelerated and rammed into the back of my master's car. The car skidded to the edge. I do not know if the brakes snapped as I watched the car plunge down into the ravine below.

But unexpectedly, as the car tethered at the edge of the road, I saw the passenger-side car door swing open. The little child was flung out and landed on the side of the road.

By now, I was out of my mind in fear, remorse, and alcohol, but even in that mental condition, I could not make myself leave that poor child alone in the pouring rain.

I stopped my vehicle and picked up the child.

I was not thinking; I acted on impluse as I set off once again with the little child inside.

I drove down frantically past two sleepy towns before sanity returned, and the gravity of the situation dawned in my addled brain. I was to drop off the vehicle in the next big town, the gem city of Ratnapura. When my predicament of being seen with the little child hit me. I diverted off to another route, heading south. This was a less travelled, lonely route, and after some time at a place that was deserted, I stopped, carried the little child, sat him on the side of that road, and left him there.

It was nearing midnight; the skies were dark with heavy clouds. I hoped the child would be safe, but it was myself, I was more worried about as I turned my vehicle around and headed back towards the gem city of Ratnapura.

When I reached the town, it was well past midnight. I parked the lorry at the given location, replaced the keys as I had found them, and walked to the town's main bus stand. At that late hour, I encountered not a single person as I sat at the stand in the cold, shivering in shock and fright. In the early hours of the morning, I boarded a bus heading to the city of Kandy and proceeded from there to my village.

When the tragedy came to light, I was genuinely very ill. Even as I was questioned by the police, I was running a high temperature and could hardly hold up my head. Many guests had witnessed my early departure from the venue due to my ill health that night. People had vouched for my presence on the journey back on that bus in the early hours of the morning. I maintained I had hitched a ride in a passing lorry to get from the venue to the bus stand. My illness was apparent to all as, at the time, I was both mentally and physically sick.

The sad occurrence that night was ruled as a tragic accident. The car had fallen deep into the ravine and was impossible to retrieve. The bodies of the young master and his wife recovered, the absence of the body of the little child explained as being flung further into the deep ravine and impossible to retrieve.

The funerals were attended by thousands, but I was too ill to attend. I was burdened by immense guilt for my involvement in this terrible crime. I took to drowning every memory of that night by drinking liquor heavily. The villagers sympathised and excused my sorry state as they believed my immense grief was caused by remorse at leaving the young master to navigate the unfamiliar roads by himself.

Weeks went by, guilt ate at me, and only by drinking liquor could I drown out my sorrow at the tragedy I had been instrumental in causing. The fate of the little child weighed heavily on my conscience. The face of the little child appeared every night in my restless sleep to haunt me. Liquor made it impossible to resume my former job or life. I spent my days in a drunken stupor or in troubled sleep.

I do not know why I never disclosed the survival of the little child to Mallika. I never spoke to anyone about the child.

I think, by carrying out this diabolical plan of Mallika, I finally broke the power she had over me. Any link of loyalty I felt disintegrated. She mattered no more.

Mallika herself could not suppress her secret elation at the success of her manipulation. She bided her time. Months later when the tragic event had receded from people's conversations and memories, she travelled once more to Kandy to consult that same lawyer who had advised against fighting for her dues many years ago.

The marriage certificate had been legally registered and deemed legitimate. This time the lawyer felt she had a legal right and thus she set upon the next step to lay claim to her beloved Kaluwara Maligawa.

Chapter Twenty-Three

The Black King/Mohan

Mohan

Second bed, second best, could well be penned to describe my arrival at birth. I grew up as a child utterly confused as although I grew up addressing Martin as 'thaththa', as he was believed and accepted as being my father, my mother kept filling my head with the crazy idea of a lofty birthright.

My life, as I recall, can be divided into two different and distinct spheres.

As a child, I grew up in a tiny house, badly in need of repair.

An ordinary village boy running around with the other boys in my neighbourhood, too young to understand social stigma and the underlying currents relating to interactions between social classes.

My father was a kind and simple man who provided me with basic food and clothing. My mother was far from simple. She was a complicated woman and the forceful, dominant partner in that union. Although Thaththa was the breadwinner, he was a shadow in the background, completely under the rule of my mother's thumb.

My mother rarely left the house, and when on a few occasions I had accompanied her around, I found most of the villagers shunned her, and I had heard her being verbally abused by a few women.

The great tragedy that occurred to the family that lived in the big Maligawa up on the hill is etched clearly in my mind. In my seven-year-old mind, the policemen visiting our little house were both exciting and terrifying, and I had a vivid memory of that time. Yet, an even more terrifying recollection was the sound of hearing my mother's manic laughter echoing through our small house upon hearing of the tragedy.

It was after that fateful, tragic night my father changed from a simple, hardworking man into this dark, silent person. He spent most of his day lying comatose in bed, reeking of cheap liquor.

The man who had left every morning cheerful and enthusiastic to work was no longer employed. He never touched the wheel of a vehicle again, and my mother and I were left with no means of support.

A few months after the tragedy, I recall being taken by my mother to the nearby town of Kandy. I remember being seated outside poky little offices for hours on end while she met with lawyers. After a few of those journeys, I remember a particular old lawyer who visited our house. It was on his first visit that I remember being sent out on an errand. The visits occurred regularly, and each time, I remember being told to leave as they had important legal matters to attend to. Some days, she left with him, professing court appearnces and returning a day or two later. At that young age, it did not occur to me how we got by without my father's wages. It was only when I was older it struck me that my mother had resorted to her usual practice of enticing a man with her physical charms as a means of survival.

Memories of our house being pelted with stones and my mother being verbally abused on the roads linger. I was no longer welcome at neighbourhood homes, even the ones that had tolerated my presence earlier, in spite of my mother's notorious reputation.

I attended a village school, and as most children mimicked their elders, I bore the brunt of being picked upon or bullied by the older students, while others were forbidden by their parents to associate with me. The most commonly used term of 'a whore's son' is ingrained in my memory.

As the years rolled by, my mother's periodic visits to attend court became clearer to understand, and as I grew taller and bigger with age, it became easier to withstand the physical assaults on me. I was not a good student academically, and in my early teens, thankfully being physically larger than other students, I began to subdue other students who dared to challenge me. I ganged up with a few other boys who were similarly aggressive in nature and not inclined to study, and we often played truant and wandered around the village, pilfering fruits from neighbourhood gardens or small items from market stalls and shops.

At the end of my sixteenth year, I entered the second sphere of my life. It was on a day when, freshly attired in a new shirt and long trousers, I accompanied my mother once again to the courthouse. After a long, drawn-out court proceeding, the verdict was read. After years of arguments from rival claimants, the court deemed that my mother's marriage to Kalu Kumaraya was legal and ruled in her favour. She had now been declared as the rightful owner of his properties, but most importantly to her, her beloved Kaluwara Maligawa.

When we moved up the hill and into Kaluwara Maligawa, we moved up in life. I was no longer the village outcast but had evolved into a hardened, tougher individual who held a grudge against all who had mistreated my mother and me.

The Kaluwara Maligawa was no longer the magnificent residence it once had been. Years of neglect had taken their toll. The roof leaked, the rooms were damp and mouldy, the furnishings dusty, and the drapes worn out and faded. Yet, although it was in this sad and neglected state, it still held its dominance over the villagers below, and it still possessed many pieces of antique furniture and artefacts of immense value within.

The sale of some of these articles of value was the means of our survival in the initial years after we moved in.

People have short memories; many of the older villagers who had strong connections and loyalty to the Kalu Kumarayas family had passed on. A new generation, a new breed of youth and villagers, lived down below. In the years that followed, the old lawyer waned out of my mother's life. He had served her purpose. The scandal and talk died down. The villagers got on with their mundane lives, and my mother resumed her previous position as the mistress of Kaluwara Maligawa.

My father continued to live his solitary life at the bottom of the hill. I assumed that my mother paid for and saw to his care. She was not one to waste her time or allow anyone to intimidate her. She employed labour from outside the district to assist and soon started to cultivate and develop the lands she now owned. Soon my mother was being recognised as head of her domain and gradually acquiring the social standing she so desperately craved.

I had now passed my eighteenth year, and with the ascendance up the hill, I had acquired a new status together with a large group of hangers-on who chose to be closely associated with me. It was a time in my life I spent with much consumption of liquor and association with the opposite sex. It also brought about, with it, an unsavoury reputation.

The times of the old feudal system of power were slowly giving way to a culture where money ruled the stakes, and my mother had big dreams for my future. She had set her eyes on power and prestige and, with that in mind, acquired herself a new paramour, a ruthless local counsellor with great political ambition. Here began my introduction to the new world of politics.

It started with simple tasks of pasting posters and rallying villagers to attend political meetings, usually with offerings of local alcoholic beverages or food parcels. It progressed to intimidation and threats against anyone with opposing rhetoric.

The local councillor, and now my mother's paramour, soon moved up in rank to become the people's representative and a member of parliament.

It was a time when the uprising in the North of the island had an effect on the racial and religious divide in the country, and the newly elected representative was adept at using the race card, thuggery, and fear to retain his position of power. Here was an area where I felt comfortable, as being of the majority race and emboldened by the goons who moved alongside me. I too, rose up the power rank. The lack of my educational qualifications mattered not; it was a time when money spoke, and money was to be made. I learned the art well, acquiring a defender vehicle and a firearm to consolidate my influential position as the right-hand man to my mother's paramour, who had by now reached a ministerial position.

I left Kaluwara Maligawa and took up residence in the capital, Colombo. Life there was exhilarating and exciting. I was a regular at the many nightclubs, bars, and casinos around. Village beauties did not interest me anymore; I sought far more sophisticated company.

As the years went by, my mother set her goals higher. She had much greater ambitious plans for me and, with it, made the acquaintance and persuaded the local liquor baron of the area to become my benefactor and financial sponsor to launch me onwards on my political journey. I needed the finances to compete, he needed influence and so the deal was done as we merged into a partnership.

My name was now well known and feared in the electorate, and in the following years, with incentives provided, threats rendered, and violence utilised, I was selected as a candidate of a particular political party to stand at the next general election. I was now well versed in the art of making deals and commissions and ready to savour the other benefits victory could bring.

I still lived a high life in the capitol, socialising with a new young crowd of privileged people, including the children of powerful political and business figures of the time.

One Friday night, at a popular bar, I saw her. I had many casual liaisons with girls in the city, but this girl was from a different league. She was the only daughter of a well-established businessman, her mother an eminent doctor, and she herself pursued a career in the legal field. She was beautiful, educated, wealthy, and far above my social status. I had got myself introduced by a mutual acquaintance and was instantly smitten. It was not just her appearance or her wealth that appealed. I was bowled over by her absolute confidence. She was cordial, even friendly, but showed no other interest.

I pursued her relentlessly in the months that followed, throwing money around in flowers and gifts to impress her, but she never encouraged my advances. The more she distanced herself, the more determined I was to win her attention.

Although my mother approved of my choice, she did not encourage the dalliance at the time because she felt it would distract me from the pursuit of political glory.

My pursuit of the girl I was besotted with was put on hold for two reasons. She left the country to further her studies in the UK, and with the end of the thirty-year-long civil war and an election looming ahead, I returned to my home and electorate to ensure my victory.

The distraction, as my mother termed it, did not determine the outcome of the general election as the very next year, with a complete swing in favour of the political party I stood for, I was elected as one of the youngest representatives from my district to the Sri Lankan parliament.

Chapter Twenty-Four

The White King/Ashane

Ashane

Loud screams echoed around my ears inside the battered vehicle when I suddenly realised it came from within and it came from myself. I had finally found my voice.

I was around seven years of age at the time and I remember it well as it was a time I was obsessed with thoughts on the arrival of 'tooth fairies'. I was seated strapped in the backseat of the car being driven by my uncle Sudath; Uncle Tony sat beside him; we were driving back to Long Island from the city of New York. It was winter time, the motorway was icy and slippery, Uncle Sudath was driving fast, and I was busy playing a game on my newly gifted 'Gameboy'. I did not notice the large container truck passing us by, I did not see it unexpectedly swerve into the lane we were driving on, but I felt it when the truck clipped our car and sent us spinning up in the air.

I do not recall much of my early childhood before I came to live in this new country I call home. I grew up with my grandmother, whom I lovingly called Mama, and I never knew my parents. After my arrival in this country, my most vivid memories are of the numerous occasions I was taken to doctors, speech therapists, and psychologists as I was nonverbal. This was up until my seventh year and the accident.

Yet, this very unfortunate accident became a blessing in disguise, for although the vehicle was a right-off and we were battered and bruised, we escaped without major injuries, and it resulted in me regaining my ability to speak.

I lived with my grandmother in a large and beautiful home in Oyster Bay, Long Island. My grandmother owned a business and worked very hard, but she always had time for me. I attended a school in my neighbourhood to which I was dropped off and picked up by Mama.

I was an introverted child, and being different and unable to communicate, I did not have friends, so I lived a lonely life. My world was wrapped around my Mama, whom I adored, and the only other people who were my companions were the two elderly uncles I possessed—Uncle Sudath and Uncle Tony. They worked and lived in New York but would drive up to Long Island most weekends. Uncle Sudath read me stories and festered in me a love of books and reading. The two uncles spent many an evening playing board games and they introduced me from a very young age to games of scrabble and chess. My early years, though lonely, were one of comfort and security, cosseted in the loving care of these three older beings.

From my early childhood, when Mama, as a successful business person, needed to travel out of state or overseas for work, I would be left in the care of my uncles. It was after one such weekend when we were returning to Long Island, that the accident occurred.

My childhood and schooling became much more of a pleasure after I regained my speech. I often have heard it said that as if making up for lost time, I transformed into an extremely talkative child and made many friends in my school and the neighbourhood. I settled well into the subsequent primary and high schools I attended. It was while in high school and through my articulate speaking skills that I was chosen to represent the school in their debating team.

Growing up in the United States, I loved baseball and basketball, and my introduction to the sport of cricket was all through my uncle Sudath. I was eleven years old when the cricket World Cup was won by the tiny island of Sri Lanka. Uncle Sudath was ecstatic for months after, and through him, I, too, came to develop a sense of pride in the nation I had left many years ago. It was at this age I began to be curious about my roots and question my origins.

Mama had spoken to me about my adoption. Still, she could never enlighten me with any further details. Although I knew she had tried for many years to solve the mystery of my appearance at the side of a lonely road, she had never discovered or determined the reason. When she was finally able to officially adopt me and return to her new homeland, she abandoned the search.

As the years passed and life's other priorities of examinations, sports, and the opposite sex took up my time, these questions retreated to the background. It was also a time of sorrow as Uncle Sudath was unwell, and it was in my fifteenth year I lost my dear Uncle Sudath.

It was at the turn of the century when Mama planned to return to her homeland with Uncle Sudaths ashes, that she decided it was time for me to visit my motherland.

Returning to this land where I was from and had never known was a revelation. Observing the lives of people in my homeland was when it dawned on me what a comfortable and privileged life I had led and what would have been my fate if my beloved Mama had not chanced upon me on that fateful night.

Mama owned two beautiful properties in her homeland. One was a colonial bungalow in the best residential area in the capital, and another was an ancestral home set amidst a coconut plantation in the south of the island. Although I was warmly received by everyone I met, I did not know anyone apart from my dear Mama and it took me a while to get adjusted to my new surroundings and to the weather.

It was an extremely hot period of time in the capital, and usually, after sunset, I ventured out of the house to walk around the neighbourhood. It was on one of those walks I met a boy of my age and made my first friend in the motherland. Ruwan was a year older, lived close by, and attended a prestigious school in Colombo. It was at his invitation I was taken to watch a cricket match in the city. This match, known to all in the capital as the 'Big Match,' was a traditional rivalry that had existed for over a century between these two schools. The atmosphere at the venue was unbelievable, and by midday, most of the spectators, including my newfound friend inebriated, swaying, swearing, and singing loudly. That afternoon, an unexpected encounter prompted my interest in my origins to rise once again.

A middle-aged gentleman approached me, swaying waywardly. He tapped me on my shoulder, saying, "Putha, you must be Sid's son; you are the picture of your father."

At the time, having downed a couple of beers myself, I brushed off the comment, attributing it as a statement made in a drunken stupor, but the statement stayed in my mind, and I could not forget the name.

The next morning, the comment was stilll on my mind. It bothered me that I had not been far-thinking enough to find out the name of that unknown gentleman who had accosted me at the grounds. This incident awoke in me the desire to find out more.

I sought out Sirisena, my grandmother's long-serving loyal driver, as she had mentioned his presence in the car the night she found me. Sirisena, in his faltering English, interspersed with Sinhalese, described the stormy night, the stops at the police stations along the way, and the subsequent visit to the hospital. However, he could not enlighten me any further in my quest for answers as none of the inquiries resulted in any identification of me.

My next lead was the mention of the name 'Sid'. Every person I asked did not recall knowing anyone by that name. I returned to the United States without a single lead to quell my curiosity regarding the mystery of my appearance on a lonely road on a stormy night many years ago.

The high school prom, college entrance examinations, and interest in girls occupied my thoughts in the years that followed my visit back to my motherland, and my curiosity about my origins was regaled to the background as I successfully gained admission to the University of Long Island to continue on with my higher studies.

In my second year at the university, I applied and successfully obtained a place at a prestigious university in the United Kingdom to follow a semester as a foreign exchange student. The United Kingdom opened up a whole new world for me, as unlike in Long Island, I came in contact with many students of diverse ethnic backgrounds, and quite a few of them were from my homeland. One such student held my particular interest.

I met Anjali while trying out for the university debating team. We developed an instant rapport with our shared interest in the subjects we were debating together with our shared origins from Sri Lanka. Anjali was beautiful, but it was not just her physical attributes that interested me; she was passionate about the social, environmental, and human rights issues we discussed, compassionate, and absolutely confident in her own abilities. I was enthralled. Thankfully, the attraction was mutual, and soon, our relationship progressed to a romantic one.

From our very first encounter at the debating stage, Anjali was convinced she had met me before, although I could not remember ever meeting her during my visit to Sri Lanka many years ago. She finally concluded she must have seen me at a distance somewhere around Colombo. My time in the United Kingdom was one of fun and joy, and I was sad to return when the year came to an end.

Anjali and I both decided to end our romantic relationship amicably, as we both felt we were not ready to commit to a long-distance relationship at the time. I returned to the United States to finish my degree, and she remained in the United Kingdom to finish hers.

I remember the year 2004 well, as it was the painful year we parted ways, and it was at the end of that very same year that disaster befell my motherland when a destructive Tsunami struck the island nation.

The aftermath and devastation caused by the Tsunami in her hometown in the south of the island compelled Mama to make the decision to return to her homeland and be of service to the badly affected coastal belt of the island.

She was in her seventies now and felt it was time to go back for good to the motherland. She sold her successful business to the successors of her former boss, rented out her palatial residence, and left to live out her remaining years back permanently in Sri Lanka.

I remained in the United States to complete my degree.

Anjali and I remained good friends and communicated often. She had returned to Sri Lanka with the intention of returning to the United Kingdom to further her studies. After my graduation, I took up an internship and remained in New York.

A thoroughly excited Anjali called me up late one night to inform me she had finally solved the mystery of her initial recognition and sense of familiarity when we first encountered each other. In a long, rambling explanation, she said it was while attending the funeral of a neighbourhood lady, who she addressed as Aunt Evangeline, that the pieces fell into place. As a child, on her many visits to this aunt's residence, she remembered an elderly domestic who resided at that aunt's house. Anjali said she used to visit the old woman in her room to listen to Sinhala folk tales as her mother chatted with her aunt Evangeline. She remembered well that on this elderly woman's bedside table was her most prized possession. It was a framed photograph of a young man who she had brought up and loved like a son. Anjali insisted that I closely resembled that young man in that photograph.

The old domestic was long gone, and the photograph was probably buried with her. With her aunt Evangeline no longer around, Anjali was none the wiser about the identity of the young man in that photograph.

Just as the funeral visit to the neighbouring house had jolted Anjali's memory, it revived in me a renewed interest in solving the mystery of my origins.

It was at the end of my year-long internship that I decided to return to Sri Lanka. My grandmother's upcoming milestone birthday, my interest in resuming my relationship with Anjali, and my desire to solve the mystery of my origins all influenced my decision to return, and so in 2007, I arrived home, back to my motherland.

When I did return in time for Mama's eightieth birthday celebration, my expectations and reality did not align as I had hoped.

I sought out Anjali as soon as I returned, but a serious relationship was not what she wanted at that time. She planned to return to the United Kingdom to complete her 'Masters' in the coming year and was not ready to enter into a long-term commitment. We resumed our close friendship, and she introduced me to her social circle and the local social scene.

In my second quest, too, I reached a dead end. Accompanied by Anjali, I visited the house of her neighbour, Aunt Evangeline, where she remembered having seen the photograph. As the old aunt Evangeline had no immediate family, the house had been bequeathed to a charity, and no one at the premises at the time of our visit held any information or knowledge regarding the elderly domestic who had resided at that residence many years ago.

Thankfully, the preparations for the eightieth birthday celebration went as planned. At the celebratory party, I first met my uncles, Mama's stepbrothers, and my only cousin. Mama had occasionally mentioned her step-siblings, but I had not met them on my first visit home. The brothers were both in their seventies, resembling each other, but their lives had taken different paths. The older of my uncles had taken to religion and the robe, and the other to the political arena and power.

As such, I learned one had obviously no offspring but the other one had a son, my cousin Anurudha, many years my senior.

My initial introduction to my uncles was cordial, and I was totally unaware of the undercurrents playing out and brought about by my presence there.

On that celebratory night, I first became aware of the pressure Mama was being subjected to regarding her properties, Ath Dhal Walawe, inheritance, and right of succession.

It was after the dinner, and when the guests started to depart, I took Anjali out for a stroll around the garden for a breath of fresh air and in the hope of rekindling a romantic moment. It was while we were walking past an open window we heard a voice raised in anger.

My knowledge of the Sinhalese language was limited but Anjali could understand it all well. Mama spoke calmly as she tried to quieten the voices of the enraged uncles. The rant involved the announcement that Mama had made on this momentous occasion, in which she mentioned that she had willed all her properties to me.

It stemmed from the premise that I was unknown and the expectation that Mama would leave Ath Dhal Walawe and the surrounding property to her own bloodline rather than an outsider.

Their objections and displeasure were made loud and clear as they believed that Ath Dhal Walawe should rightfully be willed and passed on to my cousin Anurudha.

Chapter Twenty-Five

The Closing Gambit

Mohan

Riding on a wave of jubilation as the ethnic war that had ravaged the country for thirty years came to an end, I was elected as one of the youngest representatives to the parliament from the district I contested.

The euphoria remained for many months, with victory celebrations and felicitations held both in the city and in my electorate. This recognition is what my mother had coveted all her life and was finally within reach for my mother and myself. We revelled in the glory.

It was nearly a year later when the novelty of recognition had nearly worn off, that a friend happened to mention that he had heard that the young girl I had been so enamoured with some years back had returned to Sri Lanka.

This was the time I felt it was opportune to pursue a permanent relationship. I was now 'a somebody', a person of means, one who had influential contacts and moved around in the higher social circles of the capital. I felt she would now consider me worthwhile or a privilege to be associated with.

I mentioned her return and my renewed interest in pursuing this girl to my mother. She herself was at the time on the lookout for a suitable bride for me as she felt it was the correct time for me to settle down. She was very keen on this match, for not only was this girl the only daughter of a very wealthy man, but the family were of old money, well-known, had a privileged lifestyle, and moved and belonged in the high society circles of Colombo. A world my mother so ardently wished to be accepted into.

Not one to waste any time, I called her the very next day. She spoke to me cordially and congratulated me on my victory, yet declined my invitation to meet up for dinner, laughingly saying she would see me around some time at the usual hangouts or bars we patronised.

It came as a complete surprise that very Friday night when Anjali walked into the bar holding the hand of a very handsome young man. This young man was not someone I had met before, and when I inquired around from the usual crowd we moved with, nobody was able to identify him.

After a while, to quell my curiosity, I walked up to her table to greet her, and she introduced her companion very briefly as her friend Ashane. I observed them from afar that entire night, and although they had walked in holding hands, they did not get more intimate and spent their time in deep conversation.

I was never one to give in or give up once my mind was set on anything, so I redoubled my effort to gain her attention. In the months that followed, I called almost daily, mostly to find her phone unresponsive. I had flowers and chocolates delivered, and she would acknowledge them. She was always friendly whenever she called me to thank me, but kept me at a distance and showed no interest in pursuing any deeper relationship.

The more she rejected my advances, the more determined I became to win her affection. I had many young women willing to fall into my arms, but to make Anjali my own had now become an obsession.

Anjali had stopped patronising the usual night spots where we had previously met. I did not see her around at social events, but I had heard from mutual acquaintances that she was occasionally spotted in the company of the young man I had been introduced to. So, my attention shifted to learning all I could about this elusive young man, my rival.

In my initial inquiries, no one seemed to have any information in this regard. His family, his school, and his friends were all unknown. His residence I had discovered was a palatial colonial bungalow in the best part of town.

My mother understood my great desire to overcome any opposition to get what I wanted. She, too, wished to achieve her ambition of being welcomed into the high social circles in the capital. Seeing my attempts to woo Anjali falter, she decided the best course of action was to make direct contact with Anjali's parents. With that end in mind, she cultivated a friendship with a distant relative of Anjali's mother and arranged an introductory visit to their residence with the intent of tendering an unofficial marriage proposal on my behalf to their only daughter.

My mother was right in her assumption that this was the most likely source of information regarding Anjali's new friend Ashane, as her mother gently informed my mother that her daughter had recently gotten engaged to that very same boy.

It was here my mother gathered that the boy grew up and schooled in the United States and that he had returned to found a very successful 'start-up' company in Colombo. This was not a field my mother was familiar with but she gained the name of his grandmother of southern roots who was a well-known philanthropist and associated with many charitable institutions in Sri Lanka.

When the news of the engagement was conveyed to me I was extremely upset. Emotions of jealousy and anger surfaced.

I did not like to lose, and I could not accept it.

As I, too, had minimal knowledge in the business sphere, 'southern roots' were where I concentrated my inquiries.

Initially, I did not discover much about the woman involved in charitable work other than her good name, and then I hit a goldmine.

As a newly appointed representative and backbencher in parliament, I had been introduced to another newly elected representative from the southern district. He was about ten years my senior and I now focussed my efforts on cultivating a connection. At the very next session of parliament, I followed this gentleman into the canteen and found a seat at the same table. He was a large, dark, genial person who welcomed the interaction warmly. Here started a friendship as we discovered we both had much in common and by extraordinary chance, I gathered a wealth of first-hand information regarding the background of the young man who I considered my rival.

It was initiated by my inquiry about this wealthy lady from the south who helped many charitable causes in the southern district. To my surprise, he knew her very well, as, by unlikely coincidence, she happened to be his aunt. Through my newfound friend, I learned about the young man's wealth, education, and success and recognised him as a formidable opponent.

Over many a deep conversation fortified by bottles of stiff spirits to which my new friend was partial, I learned that I was not alone in holding a grudge against this particular young man. The adoption, the wealth, the inheritance, the right of succession, and the existence of the will all spilt out over the bouts of drinking imported foreign liquor.

My newfound friend wanted this young man gone and out of the picture as much as I did.

It was not the wealth I had an issue with. I was making plenty of money granting liquor licences to my patron, the liquor baron, and all his cronies. I also made big commissions on other projects I supported in my electorate along the way.

Politically too, with my loyalty to certain individuals, I was climbing up the ladder, with recent talk of being appointed a deputy minister. Yet, I lacked the social status, the education, and the polish that came with it. This was something my money could not buy.

Months went by, I occasionally bumped into Anjali and the young man at social events. I was extremely cordial and did not display any antagonism in public, but when I heard of their upcoming wedding the following year, it was hard to hold in my resentment at her rejection of my affection.

My mother witnessed my frustration and anger. She had planned and plotted my whole life to see me rise up in social circles; she understood my determination to win at any cost. She recognised the signs of the genes I had inherited from her.

It was my mother who plotted the next move. She insisted on inviting my new friend from parliament over to dinner at our residence to meet her. It was she who plied us with expensive liquor and directed the conversation in which we both aired our grievances, our emotions, our anger, and resentment to the common enemy. The envy and jealousy all spilt out and then she calmly implied the solution to both our problems.

It was my mother who planted the seeds of the evil thoughts that took root in my head that night.

Chapter Twenty-Six

Endgame

Ashane

The milestone birthday celebration over and the subsequent departure of Anjali back to the United Kingdom to further her studies saw me leaving Mama to live at Ath Dhal Walawe, settle down in the capital, Colombo, and get on with my life. I had been working on a venture with my contacts in the United States, and this was a time in my life when I concentrated all my effort on making this venture a success.

The project kept me fully occupied and with the difference in the time zones of my working hours, I did not have any time or energy to spare to socialise. As my new venture took off, I travelled overseas a few times to meet with my new business partners in the United States and I usually broke the journey in London for a few days to meet up with Anjali.

Two years flew by, I found my venture successful and it was amidst plans of expansion, looking out for suitable office premises and hiring numerous professionals that Anjali returned.

Here began a beautiful phase of my life. Anjali had missed me as much as I had missed her and we both realised our future happiness depended on us being together.

We rekindled our romance, and I worked hard on my project. My life was full and happy. As I wooed her romantically, we socialised, occasionally meeting up with friends and family and spending our time together. It was a time of joy and fun in my life.

Anjali was scouting for work in the field she had mastered when I persuaded her to join my start-up venture.

With both of us working hard and practically living together, one romantic evening, I proposed, and she accepted.

Mama loved Anjali and was overjoyed, while her parents accepted me and welcomed me into the family as the son they never had. They all revelled in making plans for a grand celebration at the end of the following year.

Engaged to Anjali, my first and only love, my venture now established and making good money, I felt on top of the world. Everything had fallen into place.

It was at this euphoric stage that, unexpectedly, my cousin Anurudha made an appearance back in my life. After our initial introduction at Mama's birthday celebration, I had met Anurudha a couple more times on visits back to see Mama at Ath Dhal Walawe.

He was a large, loud, hearty man who did not come across as overly bright. He had a reputation for imbibing hard spirits in copious quantities. He was over a decade my senior and came from a rural and very different background. We did not move in the same social circles, yet he was not a bad bloke, and I found him charming in his simple, laid-back way.

Mama had kept me abreast of his political career, mostly pushed to the forefront by his ageing ambitious father. I knew that Mama had contributed to his political campaign fund and had been informed by Sirisena that while he had lauded her charitable work in the electorate, he had also claimed credit for instigating them himself.

Mama had updated me on his elevation in life by gaining entry into the national parliament at the recent election. Anurudha had never made a social call to my residence, so it came as a total surprise when, one morning, he drove up to my house unannounced.

Over a cup of tea, the reason for this unexpected call was revealed. He wished to request that I accommodate some of his constituents as employees in my now flourishing enterprise. He did not understand or particularly care about the field of work I was involved in, and I was left to explain to him that my employees required a set of specialised skills, but I would consider a few of them to be employed for casual work as drivers or security personnel. The visit ended on a cordial note and I did not think much of that unscheduled and unexpected visit.

In the months that followed, Anurudha kept inviting Anjali and me to many official events, which we politely declined to attend. These invitations came regularly, and as we declined each one, it became somewhat of an awkward situation. One evening, he personally called to insist we attend his birthday party, to which I found it difficult to find an excuse, so we made an appearance at this grand celebration.

It was at this party that Anjali and I met up once again with an old acquaintance of hers. He too was an elected member of parliament and a colleague of Anurudha. Mohan, as I remembered him, had been an ardent admirer of Anjali in days gone by, but she had not met him in recent times. He was extremely charming and friendly as he congratulated us on our engagement and invited us to lunch with him on a future date at the parliament.

At the end of that same year, Anjali and her parents left Sri Lanka to attend the wedding of a close relative of her family in New Zealand. Since they had not travelled to that part of the world, they also hoped to spend a few weeks in Australia and were due to be away for about three months before they returned.

It was around three weeks after Anjali left, Anurudha visited me once again with an invitation.

This time it was for a holiday break for four or five days out of Colombo. I really did not know why I even considered the invitation, but it was a time when Thanksgiving was being celebrated in the United States, and with the coming of the Christmas holidays, a time my work schedule was less demanding. With work reduced, I had some free time on my hands. With Anjali away and my Mama busy with yet another event for charity, I was at a loose end myself and feeling a trifle lonely, so this invitation to relax came at an opportune time. For Anurudha, too, with the parliament sittings prorogued, it made it a good time to take a break.

The few days planned out were to Mohan's residence in the hills near the city of Kandy. I was still contemplating my acceptance when Mohan called me personally to invite and persuade me to visit his home. Mama and Anjali were both in favour of my holiday out of town, as they felt I needed some company and a small break. It also was an instance I could alleviate my guilt at declining most of Anurudha's invitations before.

Mohan's ancestral residence was imposing and impressive, the interior was ostentatious but comfortable. There were two other couples and a young girl at Mohan's residence when Anurudha and I arrived on a Friday evening. I assumed the pretty young girl was Mohan's girlfriend, but from the moment I arrived, I was made extremely uncomfortable by her unwelcome advances and too familiar attention, which I ignored. The couples were staying over for the weekend, making the company more diverse, the conversation varied, and the weekend was spent relaxing with interesting topics being discussed. One of the gentlemen there was an official from the archaeological ministry and one evening, the conversation centred on a particular place in that electorate, which in recent times had been of great archaeological interest. It was a relatively undiscovered cave, set high on a local mountain range, and yet to gain attention from the general public.

After a sedentary weekend with much food and drink, the hike to this cave was suggested by Anurudha and so the excursion to this archaeological site was planned for the following day. We set off very early the next morning. The excursion party consisted of Mohan, Anurudha, the driver, and myself.

It was a two-hour drive to the spot from where we commenced our climb, and initially, the track was a relatively easy one. It was around ten that morning when we reached a beautiful water spot where Mohan suggested we take a break, have a rest, and partake of the breakfast that the driver had been recruited to carry along. The climb to the cave after was deemed to be steep, difficult, and more dangerous. After breakfast, Mohan handed me a welcome cold lime juice to drink.

About half an hour after we commenced the second stage of the uphill climb, I started feeling light-headed, but I did not give it much heed as I thought it was the elevation that caused it. We had now arrived at the dangerous section of the climb, a narrow path at the edge of the cliff we were ascending with a steep drop on one side.

Looking down made my head spin, and I felt dizzy, but there was no turning back as the path was too narrow.

Mohan was just ahead of me, the large and burly Anurudha behind, with the driver making up the rear. I heard Mohan assure us that the cave was just ahead when, at a particularly narrow spot, he made a sudden stop to turn back, taking me by complete surprise. I bumped hard on him, stumbled, lost my balance, and teetered at the steep edge. I tried to reach out to Mohan to break my fall but he had moved well back. I tumbled over and everything went black.

Chapter Twenty-Seven

Checkmate

Agnes

I awoke with an uneasiness, a premonition of doom. I tried calling Ashane throughout that morning with no success. He usually called me every morning, a practice he followed from the day I had gifted him his first phone in his teens. There was a heaviness that weighed upon me as I waited for his daily inquiry into my health and programme for the day. Getting no response from his number, I anxiously tried to get hold of Anurudha, but to no avail; his phone was switched off.

When Ashane told me about the invitation, I did not dissuade him from accepting it. I was ageing, and I thought it would be good for Ashane to be on cordial terms with the only relative he would possess when I was no more. Yet this morning, something did not feel right. I felt it in my bones, a foreboding of disaster.

I was usually not swayed by feelings or emotions, and I had a strong will, but regarding my beloved Ashane, I was weak and near breaking point when that afternoon Anurudha called.

I strongly believe that three factors saved his life.

The gods decided to spare him as a reward for every prayer and charitable act or donation I made or had carried out in his name. A sturdy strap of the backpack he had been wearing struck and held on to a gnarled root protruding out of that steep cliff. The young driver, who had not waited for instructions or hesitated an instant, 'he turned and ran down' the steep path to alert the villagers below.

The villagers, who were familiar with the terrain and had the necessary tools, spikes and ropes, subsequently carried out the rescue.

Ashane had bumped and struck a few boulders on his descent before the miraculous intervention of the sturdy strap and root that had saved his life. He had broken bones in his legs and arms, but thankfully, his skull or spine had not been affected.

He was carried by the villagers on a makeshift stretcher to the closest rural hospital from which the young doctor there had advised against any further movement to observe for any internal bleeding.

I travelled that very afternoon to reach the remote rural hospital to find my beloved Ashane, scratched, bruised, broken bones, and heavily sedated but still breathing and alive. Mohan and Anurudha were present at the hospital, and Mohan insisted I stay at his residence as it was the closest place in the vicinity of the rural hospital. It was here I stayed and visited Ashane daily to monitor his recovery.

It was around ten days later that Mohan and Anurudha returned to the capital and Mallika, Mohan's mother, arrived to take care of me and Ashane. After two weeks at the rural hospital, arms and leg heavily plastered, face bruised and bandaged, and groggily conscious, Ashane was carefully transferred to Kaluwara Maligawa, where Mohan insisted we stay until Ashane was sufficiently mobile to be moved to Colombo. Mohan and Anurudha were in constant touch and very concerned during the time of Ashane's recuperation.

As the days went by and with Ashane mostly sedated, I had plenty of time on my hands. I was never one to be idle, and being interested in family history and ancestry, I inquired if there was any recorded information regarding the history of this Walawe and the family. Surprisingly Mallika was quite unaware of the family history and proffered ignorance of ancestors before her late husband, yet she obliged by letting me dig up some old albums to peruse and while away my time. The dusty old albums buried in an old ebony cupboard seemed to have lain there untouched for decades.

It was in one old album I came across old photographs in black and white print with images of figures who seemed familiar. At first, the familiarity did not connect, but it subsequently struck me that the facial features uncannily resembled my Ashane.

I really don't know why I withheld that information about the resemblance from Mallika. I commandeered one photograph of a young man who held a remarkable resemblance and started secretly inquiring around about the families who had previously resided at Kaluwara Maligawa.

The immediate household staff were not persons who were of the area or village and knew very little of any previous occupants so I decided to venture further afield and into the surrounding village below and make discreet inquiries while making general conversation with the villagers. It was at the local Sunday market fair I found an initial source. This old woman had lived in the village long enough to enlighten me on the scandalous nature of Mallika's relationship with the previous owner, Kalu Kumaraya, but the photograph I showed of the young man brought no recognition. It was from another old woman who was around that Martin's name cropped up.

Martin, I was told, was the best source of information regarding the family and the tragedy that befell them.

Martin, I was told, was a man who dwelt in a ramshackle house at the bottom of the hill, immediately below the Maligawa. When I asked around, I heard that Martin was a lost cause, not quite right in his head, and addicted to the local moonshine, yet in recent times, people did mention he had forsaken alcohol and taken to religion.

Gaining access to Martin without raising undue attention presented a problem, but Martin's recent interest in religion and my reputation for taking up charitable causes helped as I looked for a way to make a connection.

I first recruited a young local priest to visit Martin, and after a few visits, I offered through the priest and my charitable trust to help repair the leaking roof of that ramshackle abode. Offers with financial gain were something Mallika was loath to refuse, and soon, I had arranged for the workmen to carry out repairs. With the workmen within and the priest visiting daily, I now had reason to venture into the house at the bottom of the hill.

Martin, the old driver, was a weak, feeble man who lay in one corner, lost to the world. In the next couple of weeks, with my daily visits to view the work in progress, Martin gradually got used to my presence in the house. He would, on occasion, enter into some conversation mostly on religious lines. One morning, on introducing the subject of the Moonemalle family, Martin became visibly agitated and turned away and spoke not a word. On the next few occasions, I mentioned the family and the tragedy, but I had no success; Martin clamped up and retreated to his own world. I was near to giving up when I decided to bring with me the photograph of the young man I had found in the old album.

It was on the day he saw the photograph that I had left by his chair, I saw him break down. The poor man was visibly upset, tears streamed down his face as he rambled incoherently about retribution and punishment in his afterlife. It was to the young priest that he had eventually identified the young man in the photograph as his last employer and the previous owner of Kaluwara Maligawa.

I knew I was on the right track but Martin did not reveal any more information for me to proceed in my search for answers.

It was nearly six weeks after that fateful accident, and thankfully, Ashane was in much better shape. The bandages around his face were removed, and cuts and bruises receded. The doctors had mentioned that in another two weeks, he would be able to have his casts removed and return to Colombo.

It was around the same time Anjali and her family were due to return. I had informed Anjali about the accident at the time, but at Ashanes' insistence, I had not given her details of the gravity of his injuries since he did not want her to cut short her trip and return. Being away from the capital had its advantages, as having privacy helped keep the details to a minimum.

After spending over a month in bed and now almost fully recovered, he often joined me on my long drives around the surrounding areas to relieve the monotony of being laid up and immobile in bed for so long. Late one morning after one such outing, I decided to stop at Martin's house to have a word with the workmen regarding another repair that needed to be attended to. Ashane felt he needed to stretch his legs and decided to hobble along to see 'my holiday project', as he termed it. I was not prepared for the outcome and the breakthrough the visit provided.

Martin was awake, seated in his usual spot in a corner, the young priest seated alongside with a cup of tea in his hand. The moment Ashane followed me inside, I heard the cup drop to the floor and shatter before Martin himself dropped to the floor to worship Ashane. He clung to Ashane's plastered feet and begged for forgiveness.

Ashane, quite taken aback, extricated his feet and hastily beat a retreat to the vehicle, thinking he was dealing with a madman.

I was glad the young priest was present as Martin started to speak. It was as if a wall had been broken, as in absolute frenzy, he finally opened up and related the part he played and the dastardly deed he carried out on that fateful tragic night. Although the gist of the tragic event was coherent, the story was disjointed. I heard Mallika being mentioned in it and understood parts of it, but the ramblings about a little child were what pricked my interest and curiosity.

Thankfully, the young priest was not from the village and was totally unaware of the tragedy that occurred so many years ago. He just witnessed the agitation, the erratic rambling, and the calls to retribution and redemption, so it was easier for me to get the young priest to make the case to Mallika of removing Martin to a nearby hospital for a few days.

A few days later, I visited Martin at the rural hospital to find him still agitated, muttering unintelligibly in bed. When I returned to Kaluwara Maligawa, I informed Mallika that Martin needed psychiatric help, and I was willing to bear the cost of transferring him to Colombo.

I knew Mallika was one who would take up any financial offer. Mallika, over time, may have gotten complacent over her actions of years ago; she may have blocked the event from her memory and did not sense any threat from Martins's removal to the hospital.

She did not suspect that removing Martin from any influence she had over him was my ulterior motive, and so the next week, I arranged for Martin to be transferred to Colombo.

The time had also come for our departure from Kaluwara Maligawa. Ashane had most of his casts removed and so we bade farewell to Mallika and returned home.

With Ashane recovered, Anjali and family back, and Martin in hospital under treatment, life settled back into a routine.

It was also a time of political change. A sudden unexpected change of leadership led to both Mallika's son Mohan and my nephew Anurudha being ousted from their respective parliamentary seats. It was also the time the preparations for Ashane's and Anjali's wedding celebrations at the end of the year were being made. A time when my investigation was put on hold.

I kept a check on Martin through his psychiatrists and found he was slowly regaining mental stability, although they did not think it was still time to question him.

Ashanes and Anjali's wedding took place at the end of the year without the grandeur they had originally planned. The near-fatal accident that took place, I think, altered everyone's perception of priorities. My brothers and a subdued Anurudha attended the ceremony, but Mallika and Mohan, although invited, were notable absentees.

After my beloved Ashane left with Anjali on an extended honeymoon abroad, I concentrated on my mission to uncover the secrets I believed were linked to Kaluwara Maligawa.

Martin had been shifted into a room at this private psychiatric hospital. With the best of medication and diet, he had gained weight and looked well when I first dropped in to visit. At first, my conversations were mostly centred on religion, life, and death. Gradually, over time and months, he came to have some comfort in my company, and one day, he quietly confided he needed to repent.

It was then I organised, with his consent, the young priest, the psychiatrist, and a policeman to sit along to record his statement. Martin, by now coherent and sane, finally confessed to the evil plot devised by Mallika. The murder of the young master and his family, and the part he played in the sequence of events that led to the dastardly deed he carried out to ensure Mallika's ambition to claim Kaluwara Maligawa for herself.

But the most important information to me was the survival of the young child who he had left behind at the side of the road.

It was only I who understood the significance of this startling revelation.

With advice from high-ranking police officials, the subsequent arrest of Martin, and his confession recorded officially with a lawyer present at the police station, Mallika's arrest made headline news. Mallika was later released on bail as there was no evidence to support his accusation as it was his word against hers.

I don't think Mallika or Mohan suspected my part in the uncovering of the plot. They had no reason to connect me and Ashane to the tragic event of many years ago.

The trial, with the sensational revelations of Martin's confession and Mallika's defence and claims of Martin's insanity, dragged on for more than a year, with the main point of interest being the disappearance of the little child Martin claimed survived the accident. With the passing of time, Martin was charged with the murder and imprisoned. He was relieved to have unburdened his guilt and happy to face the consequences. Yet, Mallika, I was informed could not be charged because of the lack of evidence. With just Martin's word against hers, a man who had been under psychiatric care, his accusation was not considered enough to proceed.

It was also through political pressure that the matter was buried as with a new president, Mohan was once again in a position of power and influence once more.

It was at my instigation through the contact I had in the police department that the D.N.A. tests were ordered by the courts. The bodies were exhumed and the saliva of Mohan was submitted as I awaited the results with great interest. I had privately submitted Ashanes blood for D.N.A. tests as well.

After many months of waiting and through my contacts, I got information regarding Mohan's tests. It was established that Mohan was not the son of Kalu Kumaraya; he did not carry the genes of that illustrious family but was the offspring of Martin. Yet, with the influence wielded, the results were not released to the public.

Later, my Ashanes results reached me, and I finally knew for certain the origins of the little boy the gods had gifted to me one stormy night many years ago.

Initially, I was in a quandary as to how I should proceed. I was contemplating whether I should let the matter rest or make it known.

I knew Mallika, as Kalu Kumararayas's lawful wife, was still entitled to Kaluwara Maligawa. I was reluctant to drag my Ashane through a lengthy legal battle.

Then life made that decision for me as the pandemic took over the world. A year of isolation passed. A year the courts were shut, a year to ponder and reflect on my next move when we got the news of Mallika's demise due to the dreaded disease. With her son residing in Colombo, she had chosen to live at Kaluwara Maligawa with just two helpers during that time of isolation. I heard later that one of the domestics had contracted the virus and was sent to the hospital; the other had fled the house, leaving Mallika on her own. When she herself succumbed, she had been left to suffer and die alone in her beloved Kaluwara Maligawa.

I chose to live at Ath Dhal Walawe with my loyal staff and two trained attendants Ashane had insisted on employing.

It was a time of reflection, prayer, and peace.

I was well past the age of ninety, and my end was drawing near. I felt my age in my aching bones, and my memory showed signs of forgetfulness. I had come to a decision that Ashanes' life of peace and happiness should prevail. The discovery of his identity would remain a mystery and be buried with me.

One morning, Ashane and Anjali visited with joyous news. After many years and two miscarriages, Anjali was three months into her pregnancy. I sensed the joy and excitement in my dear boy's face, but something seemed to weigh him down. I knew him well, and when I was alone with him I inquired on what troubled him.

It was the unresolved uncertainty about 'who he was' that played on his mind. The impending arrival of an offspring had brought those thoughts to the forefront.

It was at that moment I changed my mind.

The game must play on.

Chapter Twenty-Eight

The Grandmaster

Ashane

When Mama summoned Anjali, me, and her parents to Ath Dhal Walawe the very next weekend, we were worried. Although her mind was still sharp, her body was exceedingly frail.

As we drove down anxiously early that Saturday morning, we did not know what to expect, and we were totally unprepared for the bombshell that dropped on us.

After breakfast, Mama was ready to greet us. She was not lying in her bed as we expected but seated at a desk with two files laid out in front of her. As we gathered around, she spoke slowly, gently, but clarly. She related the sequence of events to the tragedy and revealed the secret of my identity.

In those files she possessed were copies of Martin's confession, photographs, and D.N.A. reports to substantiate her story.

All my life, from the day I had first asked Mama about my father and mother, and she had gently revealed the circumstances that led to her possession of me, I had always wondered who I was. No matter how much my dear Mama adored me, I had always harboured a feeling of insecurity about being abandoned by my own parents. I realised early that I was one of the lucky ones, a boy who always had people who loved and nurtured him, educated him, and gave him everything he materially desired, but there was always something about my life that felt incomplete.

When Mama revealed the facts, everyone was shocked and in tears over the devastating tragedy of my parent's murder, but after the initial emotions had worn off, I was thankful for finally learning the truth.

Mama requested the others to leave, and with only me at her side, she handed me the files. She explained why she had not told me before; she admitted her reluctance to disrupt my happy life, and she said it was withheld through love for me. She hugged me close and said I was the greatest blessing she had received in all her life, and she loved me with all her heart.

I think the dilemma she was under about divulging this information had kept her lingering on, as that very same night, Mama peacefully closed her eyes and passed on.

The next few months passed in a blur. The funeral, the crowds that visited to condole, the prayers and the lawyers, the will and inheritance, and most importantly, the birth of my son took up my time and thoughts that the revelation of my identity did not matter as much.

Yet I could never forgive or forget.

Anjali and her mother were both of the opinion that now that I knew my heritage, I did not need the possessions to prove my worth, but my father-in-law felt justice needed to be done, and I could not and would not let it rest.

The country was facing hardship; the political climate was volatile at the time. The once-powerful politicians were facing immense unpopularity, and the public was demonstrating their displeasure; times were changing once again.

There were two reasons that fuelled my desire to proceed.

The first was personal. The birth of my son made me realise that even though I had been denied the right to the name, my son had every right to claim his birthright; he should not forgo that right.

The second reason had always rankled in my mind, but I had never acknowledged that suspicion or spoken to anyone about it. I had always felt that my near-fatal fall had not been as accidental as everyone supposed. Mohan's sudden stop to turn, the deliberate bump and most decidedly his step back from my outstretched hand was something I had replayed many times in my thoughts of that fateful day. Now, with the revelations of the evil plot and deed carried out by Mohan's parents, I was more than convinced it had been pre-planned.

Of my cousin Anurudha, I was still uncertain. He was a fool, easily manipulated, and may have been merely a pawn in getting me there. The reason was unclear; maybe Mohan had been aware of who I was and the threat I could be.

At my initial inquiry, I found Kaluwara Maligawa was now sealed and shut. Mallika had succumbed to the virus and died isolated and suddenly, leaving no will. Mallika had been legally married to Kalu Kumaraya, with the D.N.A. results of Mohan being leaked and he recognised as the son of Martin, the right of ownership was embroiled in a dispute. There were other claimants, and the matter was still being decided in the Probate court.

My father-in-law hired the best of lawyers as I staked my claim.

With Martin's confession, he was summoned once again to courts to reconfirm his part in the tragedy, the D.N.A. results which established my bloodline, and my undisputed claim to Kaluwara Maligawa was upheld. The courts legitimised the rightful ownership of my name, Kaluwara Maligawa, and all its property belonged to me.

Mohan left Sri Lanka and relocated to distant Canada. I never heard from him or of him again. Anurudha remained back in the village. The country was going through a difficult period of hardship and he was no longer in the political fold.

I lived happily in the capital, Colombo, with my wife and son, who proudly carries the name of my dear father and Mama—Siddhartha Moonemalle Wijenayake.

Kaluwara Maligawa is now run as a home for abandoned children. Mama's ancestral home and property Ath Dhal Walawe is leased out and is now a renowned boutique hotel in Sri Lanka.

On quiet nights, I often ponder on this game we all play on this chessboard we call life: What would have been my life if tragedy had not befallen my parents? What path would my life have taken if the angel I called Mama had not come upon me on that lonely road on a stormy night?

Did I emerge a winner, or did I lose in life?

Am I the Grandmaster, I wonder?

Glossary

CHAPTER ONE

1. Holman - Ghost

CHAPTER TWO

1. Moonstone - elaborately carved semi-circular stone placed at the bottom of the steps to entrances. It is a unique feature of the architecture of ancient Sri Lanka

2. Maduwa - an outer area or building, usually at the rear end of a residence

3. Ath dhal - elephant tusks

4. Walawe - heritage homes

CHAPTER THREE

1. Kralls - enclosure where wild elephants are driven to be tamed.

2. Perahera/parade or procession.

CHAPTER FIVE

1. Sudhu - White

2. Baba - baby

3. Nona - lady

4. Kumari - princess

5. Ayah - a native term for a nanny for children

CHAPTER SIX

1. Paddakama - a piece of traditional jewellery usually worn by brides in the Kandy district of Sri Lanka

CHAPTER EIGHT

1. Malay - an ethnic group belonging or relating to origins from the country Malaysia

CHAPTER ELEVEN

1. Maha Gedera - family home

2. Buggy cart - a small cart usually drawn by a horse or bull

3. Loku Nona - Lady of the house

4. Loku Hamu - Lord of the Manor or house

5. Podi Hamu - Junior master of the house

CHAPTER TWELVE

1. Rate Mahattaya - a traditional title from the Kandyan Kingdom, which became a part of the British Colonial administration.

2. Kodavina - evil charm

3. Hooniyan Kappana - ceremony of breaking an evil charm

CHAPTER THIRTEEN

1. Kaluwara - Ebony

2. Maligawa. - Palace or Castle

CHAPTER FOURTEEN

1. Kalu - Black

2. Kumaraya - Prince

3. Achchi - grandmother

4. Duwa. - daughter

CHAPTER TWENTY-THREE

1. Thaththa - father

CHAPTER TWENTY-FOUR

1. Putha - son